There was no sound save the thrust of the engines and the splash of water. Dawn was approximately two and a half hours away. The pilot's face, visible through the glass, betrayed a look of intense concentration. When he saw Harry making his way around the deck, he slid the protective glass so he could fire the Smith & Wesson gripped in his free hand.

But Harry had anticipated this. He had only brought his head into view, providing just enough temptation to impel the pilot to react. Harry slipped back out of sight just as the Smith & Wesson discharged.

All this happened so quickly that the pilot couldn't be sure whether he had hit Harry or not. So he leaned out, poking his head into the wind.

Which was when Harry, extending his Magnum out beyond the perimeter of the cockpit, answered his fire . . .

Books by Dane Hartman

Published by
WARNER BOOKS

DIRTY HARRY #4

The Mexico Kill

Dane Hartman

WARNER BOOKS

A Warner Communications Company

DIRTY HARRY #4

The Mexico Kill

The Beginning

To the horizon there was nothing to see, nothing but a vast empty expanse of ocean. The Pacific shimmered in the late afternoon sun; the world seemed to consist only of heat and light. But to the five crewmen who labored aboard the *Hyacinth* the scorching temperature made little difference. They were accustomed to working in such conditions. For years these men had been sailing the globe, generally in the pay of men like Harold Keepnews who owned the *Hyacinth*. The salt of the sea had gotten into their blood.

This leg of their journey, from the waters off Baja California up to San Francisco Bay, was a relatively easy assignment in comparison to what they had had to do the week before. Now it was a matter of navigation and keeping the craft in seaworthy shape. The fishing tournament was a thing of the past, a triumph arduously earned over a series of grueling days. The fish had made them sweat and caused them to strain and rip muscles. The fish had lost, but they'd exacted their price.

Keepnews had returned by private jet to his home, leaving his crew to bring the *Hyacinth* to him. It was a beautiful vessel, a forty-five-foot cutter with round-bilge hull and skeg rudder; a commanding presence, its towering main and foretriangle sails gave it the look of a pure white specter when viewed from a distance.

Occasionally a whale would be sighted, a gray hump-back playfully emerging from the deep, spouting a geyser of water, then vanishing again. From time to time, too, the men would observe a school of dolphins migrating in a southerly direction. But only seldom would they ever see another boat which was why, toward dusk on the evening of July 8th, the appearance of a thirty-foot cruiser bobbing listlessly in the water excited the attention that it did.

The cruiser, silhouetted against the westering sun, was visible from the port side of the *Hyacinth,* and the way it cast from side to side caused the *Hyacinth*'s skipper to think it was in some kind of difficulty. He directed the yacht to move closer to the disabled vessel.

When the *Hyacinth* drew in toward the cruiser, the crewmen began to make out a signal beacon that they'd failed to notice before with the sun in their eyes. Tiny discharges of red light were barely discernible. There was, however, still no sign of human life on board this boat whose bow declared its identity in small black letters: *Angel Lily.*

The skipper took hold of a megaphone and called out to the *Angel Lily,* asking if there was anyone on board. Presently a figure popped up from below deck, a man with straggly russet hair that drooped to his shoulders.

"Yessir, you could be of help to us," the man shouted. "Something's fucked up with our fuel, can't figure out what the hell it could be. Been out here must be two days doing circles waiting for somebody to come along. Don't know how happy we are to see you."

Something about what this man said disturbed the skipper, a fifty-year-old veteran of the sea, but he couldn't determine what it was. It sounded to him like this man and his companions, whoever they might be, didn't know the first thing about sailing. How else would they have ended up here in the middle of the Pacific, stranded because they ran into some sort of problem with their fuel? But maybe it was just the man's looks that bothered him? He was as unkempt and slovenly in appearance as the *Angel Lily*. The *Hyacinth*'s skipper could sense from just cursory observation when a boat was the victim of neglect or simple abuse, and there was no question that the *Angel Lily* had suffered from both.

Despite his reservations, the skipper was not about to abandon a stricken boat. He gave the order to drop anchor, then returned his attention to the *Angel Lily*.

Now there was a second man on the deck. He was taller, less hirsute, but the skipper didn't like his looks any better. The skipper kept quiet, maintaining a steady, scrutinizing gaze, his arms crossed over his chest.

"We got a dinghy here, we'll be over there directly," said the first man.

"Don't you want us to come over to you?" the skipper inquired. "Maybe we can diagnose your problem and send you on your way."

"Oh, save yourself the trouble. No way in hell this crate's going to get anywhere. Needs a major overhaul. And it's sure not worth it. You just take us partway up the coast we'd be mighty appreciative. Drop us off a bit south of Ensenada be just fine."

The first mate was dubious and expressed his sentiments to the skipper who felt exactly the same way. "But I don't see what else we can do really. After all, we can't just leave them here. Ensenada is not far from Tijuana. By tomorrow afternoon we can get rid of them."

The mate was compelled to agree with the logic of this, without, however, being any more convinced of its wisdom.

"We just have to load in a few things here, and we'll be right with you folks. Don't want to hold you up none on account of us."

After several minutes had passed, the two men carefully lowered their inflatable dinghy over the side and then clambered into it. The dinghy, luridly orange against the darkening water, seemed to take forever to reach the waterline of the *Hyacinth*.

The yacht's crew members assisted the two in hoisting up their duffel bags, which were as bulky as they were

9

heavy. "What in God's name have you got in those things?" the skipper asked.

The bearded character, who was the only one who seemed to do any talking, shrugged, replying, "All sorts of junk, nothing special."

With the two safely on board with their possessions, the skipper ordered the anchor lifted. Preparations began to maneuver the *Hyacinth* back on course. By this point, the crew was too preoccupied to pay much more than perfunctory attention to the new arrivals. They were given berths and provided with food and drink; that was sufficient, in the skipper's view, to satisfy the demands of seagoing hospitality.

Overhead the sky was filling up with stars, becoming glutted with them. Some of them refused to stay put and went streaking crazily downward, looking as if they had every intention of plunging into the Pacific.

Two of the crewmen had decided to retire. The three others, including the skipper, remained on deck, guiding their craft north against a gentle five-knot wind. What the two strays they'd picked up were doing they had no idea; presumably they'd gone to bed. They'd heard not a sound from them since they'd come on board.

In the silence, broken only by the sea lapping against the hull, any noise, even a cough or a grunt, was easily picked up, and it sounded louder, more significant than it actually was. When the three men on deck heard the footsteps, bootheels producing a rough rhythmic tattoo against the stairs that led from the cabin—they all turned around to see who was coming.

It was their two guests.

"Anything we can do for you gentlemen?" the skipper asked, still looking out toward the sea rather than at them.

"Not a thing," responded the bearded man. "Not one blessed thing."

The first mate started to say something. But he sputtered his words, and they weren't articulate enough for the skipper to adequately comprehend.

10

Nor did he have an opportunity to make himself understood.

Just then there was a terrific clatter and a burst of blazing light that for an instant outdid anything in the sky. Then the first mate tumbled over, his chest torn apart and becoming engulfed with blood. The skipper turned and beheld two AK47s confronting him. He did not know whether first to protest, appeal for mercy, or demand an explanation. In any case, he was not given a chance. Two Soviet-made machine guns were trained on him simultaneously. One took him to the port side, the other to the starboard. Bullets from one gun met and coupled with bullets from the other midway in his body. Spun into the air, a man twice, three times dead, he crashed into the sea that he'd sailed all of his life. The third crewman, immobilized by the fear, made a belated attempt to run. The problem was there was nowhere he could go, no escape. A single shell trapped in the base of his neck was sufficient to kill him. Others followed, but they were simply gratuitous.

All this commotion had predictably aroused the two crewmen below. The hijackers were prepared for them. As they raced up the stairs they were met by a withering fire that tore into both of them, sending them reeling back down into the cabin, their bodies gaping grotesquely with holes that rapidly filled with blood. For a few moments, an arm could be seen moving in the tangle of limbs and bodies, flailing this way and that. But the man was dead and simply hadn't realized it yet.

The two assailants, their clothes spattered with the blood of the men they'd so easily killed, regarded their night's work with satisfaction. "Two for the price of one," the bearded man remarked.

"Never mind that," the other muttered. "Time to dump them overboard. The sharks are waiting for their supper."

Chapter One

Harold Keepnews was not a man who liked to be kept waiting. He had not amassed forty million dollars by waiting. In fact one of the reasons he'd gone out of his way to make so much money was so that he wouldn't have to endure long lines and endless delays. If someone told him that he would get right back to him, well, he assumed that he would. No one put off Harold Keepnews.

Maybe it was all that money that made him look as prosperous and as vital as he did, but you never knew. He had the sort of presence that commands respect. He sauntered into a room, and you knew right away that whatever he did it must be something truly important. Determined to fight back the encroachment of time, he exercised regularly in a gym he had built onto the back end of his house, ate vegetarian, drank herbal teas, and voted Republican. The Democrats he was sure would drive him and his friends into penury before long.

You had the feeling Harold Keepnews would live a long time no matter what party controlled the White House. His granddaddy had made it to the venerable age of ninety-one, his father had succumbed two months shy of eighty-nine. They had passed on to Keepnews a handsome genetic legacy.

Keepnews had friends everywhere, friends in the police, friends in the Coast Guard. Which was why he assumed that his problem would be very quickly, and smoothly, ironed out.

"My boat's been hijacked," he declared matter-of-factly to Captain Cornell Haines who was trim and handsome enough to have walked right out of a Police Benevolent Association poster. Keepnews didn't like to sound alarmed even though the circumstances might be pressing.

Haines had met Keepnews on a variety of occasions, official ceremonies mostly at which San Francisco's social and financial elite was expected to turn out. Keepnews was the sort of man who didn't have to look into a mirror to remember what he looked like; his photograph was in the newspapers that often.

Haines respected Keepnews and listened carefully to what he was saying, taking notes. He didn't have to take many notes though. Keepnews preferred to be succinct.

"When did this happen, sir?"

"Sometime between the 5th of July and yesterday. I couldn't tell you exactly when."

"How do you know that the *Hyacinth* wasn't simply lost at sea? There's always the possibility of an accident. I'm not suggesting that you're wrong, sir, I just want to explore all the options."

Haines looked up at Keepnews, fully expecting a reprimand for his presumption. He'd much rather have conducted this interview at the station than here in the lush airy setting of Keepnews' house.

"It was no accident. If it were an accident I'd be talking to my insurance agent now and not you. We are talking about piracy and murder."

Haines didn't like the sound of the word piracy. It had a vaguely anachronistic ring to it. On the other hand, it wasn't such a farfetched allegation. People were crazy if they didn't take a 30-30 or a shotgun with them when they set out on sea journeys of any significant distance. It had gotten that bad. But Haines was strictly a city boy. What happened in the water—unless that water was the bathtub water somebody drowned in—was none of his concern. Still, when a man like Keepnews talked you listened.

"You must admit, Mr. Keepnews, that if your charges are true, and they may well be. . ."

"There should be no doubt in your mind," Keepnews broke in.

13

"It's not my mind that counts here. It's a matter of gathering evidence. You maintain no radio contact with your boat, then it disappears with all on board."

"The crew disappeared, not the boat."

Haines looked puzzled. "I'm afraid I don't understand."

Part of the problem in this exchange was that Keepnews had the habit of starting at the middle and working back to the beginning of his story, all the while expecting his listener to follow his train of thought.

"My boat's here. Right in San Francisco. Moored at the Marina Yacht Harbor."

"You saw it, you saw the *Hyacinth*?" Haines suddenly had the hope that this case might be surprisingly easy to solve.

"Of course, the pirates have changed the name. It's called *The Sojourner* now. They've done a painting job on it. Sails are all a mess of colors. Me, I only had white sails. These bastards have no taste."

"You are positive it is the same boat?"

"Positive. It's a Mariner, same design. You investigate you'll find a Perkins 62-horsepower diesel, skeg-mounted rudder, all the rigging's three-eights-inch stainless 304."

Haines wasn't sure he cared for all the technical details and he held up his hand to stop Keepnews from getting carried away.

"Now you said that you've spoken to Coast Guard officials."

"Joe Morse himself, you know him?"

"Afraid I don't, sir."

"Fine fellow, Joe. Known him for years. Useless though. He advised me to speak to you folks."

Haines nodded gravely. "You saw your boat when, yesterday?"

"Two-thirty in the afternoon. I've been down at the marina every day since Friday waiting for the *Hyacinth*."

"You see anyone on the boat?"

"Let's say there were some suspicious-looking fellows

14

in the vicinity but I can't say as whether they were with the boat or not."

"No one you recognized?"

"No, no one. Whoever they are, we travel in entirely different circles."

Haines rose, preparing to say his goodbyes. He wanted to assure Keepnews that the police would do everything within their power to bring the matter to a successful conclusion.

Keepnews frowned. "Captain," he said, "I expect immediate action. Tomorrow morning I would like a call from you to give me the latest report."

"These things take time, sir. We can't just invade a private yacht without reasonable grounds of suspicion."

"I gave you all the reasonable grounds you need, Captain."

This last remark Haines missed completely. His attention was diverted by the woman who'd just appeared in the doorway of the study. She was clad in a blue denim robe loosely gathered over a lustrous black tank bathing suit. Her long brandy-colored hair was dripping water down into her face but she didn't appear to notice. Her eyes were child-like, brimming with mirth and innocence; she looked like an updated version of Orphelia, taken out of the lake before she had a chance to sink to the bottom of it.

Keepnews observed Haines' reaction with amusement.

"Oh, I'm sorry, I didn't know you had company," the woman said.

"That's all right, dear. Captain Haines, meet my wife, Wendy."

Haines nodded in acknowledgment, wondering if you needed forty million dollars before a woman like this was a possibility.

Her smile, he thought, was enchanting.

"You'll excuse me, won't you? I have to run and change."

With that she was gone.

15

Keepnews' voice brought Haines back from the reverie Wendy Keepnews had just induced. "So you will phone me like you said, sometime tomorrow morning?"

"Absolutely," Haines said. But his mind was far from pirated yachts. All he could think about was the aphrodisiacal powers of vast amounts of money.

Keepnews had no faith in either Haines or the police force he represented; they would only claim that the matter was not in their purview and pass the buck to another ineffectual agency. No, Keepnews decided, unless Haines produced a miracle by tomorrow, he would have to seek another source of help. Very likely somebody who didn't mind resorting to unconventional, and possibly illegal, methods. Somebody who didn't mind getting his hands dirty doing it. Somebody like his old friend Harry Callahan.

Chapter Two

Just off Union Street, on Fillmore, a new discotheque called Dorthaan's had opened. With a five-hundred-dollar annual membership fee, the clientele was bound to be well heeled, the kind of fabulous-looking people who photographers kill one another to capture on film. The kind of people you never see until very late at night; what happens to them during the day is anyone's guess. Just like vampires in that respect.

Dorthaan's was not the sort of place that would appeal to Harry Callahan. It wasn't the sort of place he could afford either. He was drinking at a bar across the street, which was why he happened to be near the place. The bar afforded a nice vantage point from which to watch the parade of guests, the tuxedoed men and the silken women, proceeding up to the top of the stairs and standing underneath the canopied entrance while they produced their credentials to obtain entrance. The two men who stood guard, in uniforms bright with brass buttons, were not giants exactly, but two pygmies placed one on top the other still wouldn't reach their height.

Being off-duty, and with nothing in particular to do this sizzling July night, Harry entertained himself with the spectacle across the street. He noticed that the men were almost invariably older than the women, rich, established, and balding. About the only thing they had in common with the women was a deep healthy tan.

Harry had no reason to believe he'd recognize any of these people. But one, a man about fifty years of age, stuck out of the gathering crowd and not just because he lacked a tan. (It was hard to acquire a tan while you were doing five-to-ten in a federal penitentiary, after all.) He stuck out because Harry had been trying to run him down for the last six months or so. His name was Nicholas Cimentini, though his friends and his enemies—and they were more numerous by far—simply called him Father Nick. A shadowy figure in a shadowy world, he was heavily involved in the heroin trade, though he wouldn't take any of the drug himself, obeying the dealer's ancient law: Never do what you push.

Technically speaking, Father Nick was on probation and subject to such a long imprisonment that by the time he got out he'd be collecting Social Security. But Father Nick had not allowed that prospect to deter him. Couldn't stay away from temptation, Father Nick. Even the lowliest of low lifes on Mission knew that Father Nick had gone back in operation.

Now it seemed to Harry, watching Father Nick and his date who looked like she could be a starlet, a model, a high-priced call girl, or maybe all three, that this was a very rich and rare opportunity for him. It would have seemed this way if he hadn't had a few brews, but no doubt the alcohol heightened his resolve.

Harry was certain Father Nick was carrying. Maybe a handgun, maybe some coke he was saving for his girlfriend. But he was convinced that the man was too complacent to expect an arrest for a probation violation. And obviously an establishment like Dorthaan's was the last place he would expect to confront a police officer.

As soon as Father Nick was inside the club, Harry left the bar and strode across the street, mounting the stairs that led to the canopied entranceway like he'd been doing this for years.

The two uniformed guards held him with their eyes; they did not care for Harry's looks nor for the way he dressed. Clearly they didn't care for his presumption that he had any business here.

"Can we help you, sir?" Spoken in the patronizing manner of men who delighted in helping people by tossing them back down the stairs.

"Police officer," Harry said, flashing his identification in their faces. They weren't remotely impressed.

"You may well be a police officer," one agreed, "but that does not entitle you to free entrance to the club. Unless, of course, you are a guest of one of our members."

Harry owned that he was no one's guest.

"Then would you mind leaving, sir? This is a private club."

The guard's voice carried utter conviction; he evidently assumed that Harry would turn right around and walk away. But Harry had not been this close to Father Nick since he had testified against him in court six years before, and he desperately wanted him back in the slammer. An opportunity like this might never come again. Father Nick had a habit of fading back into obscurity. Following his trail was like following a man through the Sahara during a sandstorm.

"Problem is I do mind," Harry said almost apologetically.

The two men inched closer to each other, prohibiting Harry from advancing farther.

"Have you a warrant?" the one on the left inquired.

"No warrant. Just an overriding curiosity."

"We would not like to use force."

18

"Neither would I."

Saying this, Harry produced his .44 Magnum. He did not direct it at either of the guards. He did not have to. The very sight of the gun was persuasive enough.

Recognizing that resistance would be futile, the two guards drew aside to permit Harry to pass. "You can anticipate a visit from your colleagues, sir," one said to him.

"Give them my best when you call. Tell them it's Harry Callahan. I don't like people getting my name wrong."

If the police came after Harry, they'd have one hell of a time trying to find him inside of Dorthaan's. It was so crowded that movement in almost any direction was nearly impossible; you stood a better chance of passage in rush hour on the L.A. freeway. But even though you might be perfectly immobilized you could still see everything that was transpiring in the place. Mirrors were everywhere, on the walls, covering the high ceiling. Dancers, squashed up against one another whether they liked it or not, were reflected in an infinite number of ways; it was a voyeur's paradise. The only problem was even voyeurs can suffocate if deprived of air for long enough. And the heat was growing worse the longer Harry stood where he was, crushed in toward the bar which he thought the safest—and sanest—place to be. Across from him a grotesquely large neon penis blinked on and off in time to the thunderous disco music that bombarded you from every point on the compass, sending vibrations up your legs, causing your vital organs to gyrate against the walls of your body. It was not hard to figure out the meaning of the red neon object that produced its own mesmerizing rhythm of light from one of the upper tiers. Meanwhile, too high to burn out anyone's retinas, lasers dispatched narrow shafts of blue and amber over the heads of the writhing couples.

Five hundred bucks a year for this, Harry thought, you'd be better off blowing it at the races.

But where in this tumult could he hope to find his

quarry? Fighting his way through the mob, he did not allow his attention to wander, although the temptation was considerable. Some extraordinary-looking women dressed in costumes that clung to their bodies by little more than a couple of threads were constantly dancing into his visual field. Hard to avoid staring at them. Where did one meet women like this? Harry wondered.

At last he caught a glimpse of Father Nick—but in a mirror way over to his right. The dilemma he faced was where on the floor Father Nick was. It could be he was just seeing a reflection of a reflection. But this was better than nothing.

Father Nick wasn't dancing. Didn't look like the type anyway. No, he was standing off to the side (but which side?), conversing with another man whose fat jowly face and bulging belly suggested a life of fervent debauchery. The woman Father Nick had come in with, and the woman the jowly man had come in with, had been left to their own devices and were doing a dance with each other that might have put Salome to shame, though neither of them had a plate with someone's head on it—so far.

By the time the two women were sufficiently exhausted by their exertions, their glowing bodies slick with perspiration, Harry had managed to locate Father Nick's exact whereabouts on the floor. Wasn't easy. Magellan circumnavigating the globe for the first time couldn't have had a much harder time of it.

The two women returned to Father Nick and his melancholy fat friend with a look of anxiousness to them. Something, Harry surmised, was wrong. He shortly discovered what it was. They were hungry. Not for food. But for cocaine. Father Nick obviously was both prepared for the request and happy to please. From out of his pocket he extracted a vial filled to the brim with snow.

Even as Harry made his approach no one in the party happened to notice him. The sight of the coke was so inspiring to the four of them that nothing short of the mirrored ceiling falling in could have distracted them. Even the fat man seemed delighted.

For the fee these people were paying they expected that their privacy would be absolute, that the force of the law would be kept well out of the Dorthaan's precincts. As a result, they did not feel that they had to retreat to the rest rooms for their indulgence. Indulgence was what Dorthaan's was all about in any case.

Harry couldn't have cared less about the coke, or about its open display. The only thing that mattered was that it was in Father Nick's possession and that he was freely distributing it.

Only when he stepped into the small circle, interrupting their ritual, did his presence register. Not because of his deliberate intrusion so much as the fact that he was dressed so strangely—strangely in so far as the clientele that frequented Dorthaan's was concerned. No tux, no outrageous leather, no jumpsuit unzipped to the navel, just ordinary, drab streetclothes.

Nicholas Cimentini gazed at him with puzzlement, his brow knitted as he sought to recollect where on earth he'd seen this man before.

Harry decided to spare him the trouble. He told him his name, told him then what he did for a living, amplifying the announcement with a display of his credentials.

Father Nick still held the vial in his hand. It was impossible for him to deny that he was in possession of an illicit substance or that he was allowing others to use it. He was a man in his fifties, endowed with the kind of dignity you ordinarily expect in elder statesmen, the ones who divide up continents and peoples with a few quick strokes of the pen. His voice had a gravelly quality to it, like he'd gotten something perpetually stuck in his throat. "And so what can I do for you, Officer?" He didn't sound the least bit intimidated or worried, though the two women backed away from the cocaine right away, snorting quickly so that none of the precious flakes would slip out of their nostrils. The fat man by his side looked melancholy again.

"What you can do for me is accompany me to the police station."

21

Father Nick didn't have to ask on what charge.

Instead he said, "This is a farce. Do you have a warrant?"

"That seems to be a common question tonight. But it's not what I'd call relevant."

"This is a private club in case you haven't noticed. You need a warrant." He turned away from Harry, dismissing him.

Harry grabbed hold of him so violently that Father Nick's grip on his cocaine loosened. Much of it spilled to the floor, causing expressions of horror to appear on the faces of the onlookers. You felt that the women in particular could barely restrain themselves from diving down to sink their noses in the stuff.

"I'm taking you in, Father Nick."

Father Nick evidently didn't like being called Father Nick, not in this company anyway.

The fat man came to life, reacting with speed you wouldn't have anticipated from somebody of his bulk. A .38 stuck out of his right hand. Harry noticed it out of the corner of his eye, but refused to let it influence him. Instead, keeping his hand on Father Nick's arm, he pulled him toward him, a fisherman reeling in his catch. His action caught Father Nick off guard while at the same time putting him right in the line of fire. The fat man had to duck around to line Harry up again.

Though their female companions were loathe to stick around and watch how all this was going to turn out, they were either too panic-stricken or too high to move an inch.

You could tell that the fat man was reluctant to fire his weapon in such a crowded public place, but he was beginning to run out of options. Most of his intelligence was buried in his cumbersome flesh so Harry didn't anticipate anything very clever from him.

Father Nick's face had knitted itself into a permanent grimace. Because he was so unprepared for this he was still trying to figure out just what he should do. Mostly, he contented himself with expressing his outrage. "You

22

fuck, what do you think you're doing?" The idea that he should be busted and sent away for the rest of his life, simply for a gram or so of cocaine, was so ludicrous that he was having difficulty taking it seriously.

The fat man decided to intervene forcibly, and he stepped right in between Father Nick, to whom he evidently owed his allegiance, and Harry. It was obvious what he intended to do. He raised his gun preparatory to bringing it down on Harry's arm and breaking his grip. He did not realize that Harry was one step ahead of him. With his free hand Harry brought out his Magnum and sighted it on the fat man. The fat man thought the better of his plan and didn't do anything at all. For a few moments, while dancers gyrated obliviously around them, the men were at a standoff.

Abruptly, Father Nick conceded. "All right, enough of this shit. I'll go with you." His announcement caused a look of great perplexity to come onto the fat man's face. Harry was just as baffled as he was. He had a feeling that this surrender was mostly for show and the coldness in Father Nick's eyes convinced him he was right. Father Nick very casually nodded to the fat man. "You be good, girls," he told his female companions, all at once very jocular as though this was a little business trip he was off on.

Father Nick hadn't reckoned on the mirrors. He was watching Harry, even trying to make conversation, as they walked away. But Harry was too preoccupied with keeping the fat man in view to listen. Nothing Father Nick had to say much interested him anyway.

He wasn't surprised to see the fat man's image grow larger instead of receding in the tinted mirror directly ahead of him. Nor was he surprised to see the fat man bring his gun up. Without waiting for him to take proper aim—no sense giving him the benefit of the doubt—he pushed Father Nick to one side, almost straight into the arms of a bewildered redhead in a bright silver dress that could have put the lights in Times Square to shame.

The fat man fired. His bullet managed to shatter a

stretch of the mirror that had betrayed him, sending slivers flying in all directions. This naturally provoked a good deal of screaming in the immediate vicinity, but you had to go only a few yards in any direction and you wouldn't have noticed a thing, not with the music—a numbing little tune from Grace Jones—as loud as it was.

Harry wanted to withhold his fire for fear of hitting some hapless innocent who had come to Dorthaan's to dance, not to get shot at. But the fat man, flustered because Harry had outmaneuvered him, was not so scrupulous. He fired again. This time he struck something other than the mirror. The girl in the silver dress, having danced into the way of the oncoming bullet—being too self-absorbed in her dancing to pay attention to such things—found herself suddenly sprawled out on the floor. She dazedly picked herself up, not knowing what had propelled her through the air so unexpectedly. Then she lowered her cloudy eyes to her dress and noticed the silver was turning a bright crimson at her stomach. The pain took a while, maybe longer than usual with the drugs in her system, to make itself felt, but when it did she shrieked and collapsed, sobbing, her hands making a futile effort to collect the blood flowing from the hole in her abdomen.

By this time, Harry recognized that the fat man was so obsessed about stopping him from taking Father Nick that he would keep right on shooting. Dancers had begun to understand this too, and they were all making for an exit, many of them only barely cognizant of what the danger was—all they knew was that they better get the hell out of there.

The fat man struggled through the panicking hordes, determined to overtake Harry. Harry was at a disadvantage in that he had Father Nick to look after.

And no question, Father Nick wasn't the most cooperative person in the world. He kept trying to loosen Harry's grip and get himself swept away in the crowd. But Harry hadn't gone this far, and risked so much, to sacrifice his prey now. Each time Father Nick would attempt to free himself, Harry wrenched his arm, hard enough to practically pull it right out of its socket. The intense pain that this caused Father Nick was sufficient to subdue him for a brief interval.

Though it was possible for Harry to keep just ahead of the fat man he could not count on maintaining the distance between them for long, not with so many people pushing one another into an ever smaller space. Penetrating farther soon became impossible. The crowd formed a barrier that was not about to give way any time soon.

Now the fat man caught sight of Harry. He aimed, he fired, but just as he did so he was jostled from the right so that the bullet went off to the right as well. It impacted at the base of a real estate dealer's spine, his white tuxedo affording no protection at all. He was driven by the force of the bullet into a couple ahead of him, but because they couldn't go forward he ended up tumbling backward. He looked startled but not especially hurt; that was because the bullet had severed his spinal cord, cutting off all feeling below the waist—for good.

Harry, witnessing this, spun right around, his gun held tight in both his hands though this necessitated giving up Father Nick for the moment. He fired once. That was all that was necessary. The fat man sustained a round in his enormous belly. The .44 cartridge had to fight its way through a considerable abundance of flesh, but in spite of all that calorie-rich tissue it was more than equal to the task Harry had designated for it. In a fraction of a second it had reached the fat man's vital organs and showing absolutely no respect for them had shredded them apart and gone out the back end, leaving a hole wide enough to put your fist through. The fat man did not fall at once. He seemed, actually, to be contemplating his next move, whether to try and survive a few moments more and gamble on taking Harry out with him. But the truth was that he didn't have it in him. Much less was in him than before the .44 had hit in fact. His face no longer had such a concentrated expression on it; killing Harry was not the

25

significant issue it once was. After an absurd interval, in which he tried to right himself, the fat man placed both his hands to the end of his protrusive bloody belly and yielded himself to the dance floor.

Father Nick had attempted to take advantage of Harry's distraction, but in escaping he was no luckier than he had been when he'd tried to impress his friends by distributing cocaine. There were just too many people blocking his passage for him to get anywhere. Harry, assured that the fat man was going to cause him no further trouble that night or any night to come, spotted and caught him easily.

"You weren't trying to go anywhere, were you?" he asked politely. "I thought we had a date, you and me."

Chapter Three

Their date didn't last very long.

The following morning, before the sun had gathered enough energy to head up in the sky, Harry was summoned to the D.A.'s office. The D.A. was a political hack named Axel Nolan. He was well into his fifties but looked fit and in the best of health. While not very good at bringing criminals to justice, he could shoot nine under par on the greens he tramped with his cronies, and since he didn't expect glowing eulogies and front-page obits when he arrived at the eternal eighteenth hole, he did not much care what people thought of him. Especially if those people were named Harry Callahan.

And, in this particular instance, he had the backing of a good many both in the D.A.'s office and on the SFPD; some were high up, others were schlepps who ticketed illegally parked cars on Van Ness, and the only thing they had in common was a loathing for Inspector #71.

"That was some shit you pulled at Dorthaan's last

night," Nolan began. He could be diplomatic in his language when he thought it was necessary. He didn't think it necessary now.

"For six months we've known that Father Nick—that is Cimentini—has been distributing junk in this city. High-grade brown Mexican stuff. No one can find the son of a bitch. If I didn't get him last night, it would've been another six months before anyone got a look at him again."

Nolan wasn't interested in what Harry was saying. He kept his eyes on the portrait of the current governor that hung on the wall above his desk. Appropriately, the painting had been rendered by a hack.

"We had to let Cimentini walk," he said.

"Walk? You set the fucker free? On what grounds? He had the snow on him, we got witnesses to that. I read him his rights, not that he doesn't know them by heart by now. Went right by the book."

"Your book reads a bit differently than mine does." Nolan finally turned to face Harry. "In my book it says that in this state there is no uniform arrest act. You cannot walk up to a man simply on suspicion . . ."

"On what fucking suspicion? He had the coke out in plain sight."

"That may be. But you barged into a private club—a *private* club I repeat—not because you observed Cimentini with any illegal substance in his possession but because you suspected he might have. I don't suppose you've heard of *Kelly v. U.S.*, but in that case something similar happened. Cop walked into a restaurant and placed a suspect under custody, and while it turned out he was guilty—after a search—there was nothing the suspect was doing that was suspicious of itself."

Again Harry tried to reason with Nolan. Impossible.

"You haven't picked up the subtlety involved here, Callahan," he continued, the tone in his voice suggesting that Harry was utterly incapable of picking up subtleties under any circumstances. "You did not spot the suspect allegedly distributing the cocaine in a public place. It was

27

a private establishment and as such is like any other private establishment including a home or an apartment. As a police officer you had no right to enter without a warrant. Under questioning, both guards at the door said that you were asked for one. You ignored them and brandished your weapon, threatening both."

"I invited them to move but I did not threaten them."

"Whether you exchanged words to that effect or merely displayed a gun I think is immaterial. Mr. Cimentini's attorney reminded the court that his client was illegally arrested in terms of a recent Supreme Court decision *Payton v. U.S.* which extended the definition of what is subject to search and seizure in the privacy of one's home. I do not propose to go into my interpretation of the decision, particularly whether Dorthaan's is equivalent to a home for Cimentini. But all things considered, it was obvious to this office that it would be a waste of the taxpayers' money to prosecute the suspect for an alleged parole violation."

"Next time I'll kill the bastard," Harry muttered to himself.

"What's that?"

"Is that all you have to tell me?"

"Not all." He was gazing down at his desk blotter, seeming to study some documents collected there. "Making a questionable arrest is bad. enough, but you also created quite a furor at Dorthaan's. Half the front page of the *Chronicle* is filled with the story." He waved the paper in Harry's face. There was a large blurry photograph of people tumbling out of the club, panic and confusion written all over their pretty faces.

"I saw it."

"One man killed, a Mr. Henry Cantwell of Sonoma, a prominent insurance executive."

"That what he was? I didn't realize insurance companies were training their executives to shoot. What do they do, blow away clients who are late with their payments?"

"I would appreciate it, Callahan, if you do not inflict your sense of humor on this office." He went back to

28

announcing the casualties of last night's imbroglio: "In addition, one woman was shot in the stomach and is now in critical condition in the intensive-care unit, another man was shot and preliminary tests on him show that he'll probably be crippled for life."

"Preliminary tests should also show that I was not responsible for shooting either of them."

"Not directly perhaps. But if you hadn't decided to burst into Dorthaan's, I don't think those two people would be in the hospital this morning. Not to mention the uncounted numbers who suffered minor injuries while attempting to flee the premises."

"You ever consider the thousands of people hooked on junk? All of Cimentini's victims?"

"The problem with you is that you tend to break things down in terms of black and white. You don't consider implications, Callahan. Which is why you are being suspended from the force—pending a full investigation, naturally. If you are exonerated you will be reinstated. If not—well, I can't promise you there won't be a trial."

"When does this suspension occur?"

"As of now."

"Without pay, I assume."

"You assume right." He turned back to contemplate the governor's sad visage, indicating that Harry should consider himself dismissed.

Harry walked out slowly. After all, he had nowhere in particular to go, no deadlines to meet.

He was still numb when he reached his apartment, hadn't quite absorbed the shock. First he loses Father Nick, then he loses his job. And it wasn't even nine o'clock. It was one hell of a morning to lose all that before you sat down to breakfast.

But the truth was he wasn't hungry. Nolan had stolen away his appetite along with his job. And while he was sweating profusely and thirsty as hell he couldn't quite summon the initiative to walk to the refrigerator and get out some cold orange juice. He just sat in a chair and gazed blankly out the window.

Which was how he was occupied when, half an hour later, the phone rang.

"What is it?" Harry had no patience and wasn't in a mood to be polite.

"Harry, that you?"

"Who is this?"

"Harold Keepnews. Long time no see, eh?"

"Hello, Harold, what can I do for you?"

"Why don't you start by coming out here for a visit?"

"Any special occasion?"

"You might say so, Harry. When can you make it?"

"How about right away?"

"I always liked your style, you know that, don't you?"

"Right, Harold."

"You remember how to get up here?"

"How could I forget?"

The Keepnews' home commanded a view of the bay that was so spectacular it was nearly impossible to tear your eyes away. About the only thing that could do it was Mrs. Keepnews. Between the bright blue water, which Keepnews' mansion overlooked from the San Francisco side of the bay, and Wendy's eyes you would have a hard time knowing where to look first.

"We haven't seen you for a million years," she said when he approached the door. He'd anticipated a servant or two, not this splendidly bronzed woman who from her appearance seemed to have nothing else to do but cultivate a tan all day long.

"What a surprise," Harry said. The sight of Wendy was the first pleasant sight he'd had all day. She was as good as it was ever going to get.

"What surprise? I live here, you know." She laughed, a delightful trilling laugh.

"I didn't think I'd see you is all."

"Well, it's not like I'm a nun stuck in a convent."

Harry observed her lithe form, the soft browning body dramatized by the thin white lines of her bikini. "No," he

30

agreed, "you don't bear much resemblance to any nun I ever met."

She laughed again. She liked doing that, laughing.

Shortly, Keepnews himself appeared. Clapping Harry on the back, he invited him inside which meant parting from Wendy. Whatever Keepnews had asked him up here for, Harry thought, he couldn't imagine it would be half as interesting as exchanging pleasantries with Wendy, idly watching the parade of sailboats on the bay.

Keepnews had first met Harry on a case a long time ago. There'd been a theft; a burglar had tried making off with a cache of jewelry one night. Keepnews had stopped him by putting a bullet into the back of his head. Keepnews was a hunter and maintained an interesting arsenal of rifles and handguns. The burglar was running away when he shot him. Didn't want to waste ammunition; one bullet was all that was necessary to change the burglar's mind by eliminating a good part of it.

Harry had been called upon to investigate. The problem was that Keepnews had gone to the papers and announced what he'd done and further, recommended that every other law-abiding citizen of San Francisco, of all California for that matter, go out and buy a gun, if they didn't already have one, and use it to protect their life, their family, and their property, not necessarily in that order.

This caused something of an uproar among supporters of gun-control legislation and a large number of minority groups, who felt that Keepnews was calling for something like open warfare against any poor sucker whose only crime might be to swipe something from the five-and-ten. That had not been Keepnews' intention, but he was not a man either to repudiate his words or to clarify them. You either understood what he was talking about in the first place or you didn't, and he for one didn't really give a damn.

But the furor was such that the word came from the mayor's office to bear down hard on Keepnews in order to demonstrate to the concerned citizenry that he was not being let off easy. No one on the force especially relished the assignment. Not that they exactly condoned what Keepnews had done, but they weren't especially put out by it either. The man he'd killed had a rap sheet that read like a catalogue of the ten plagues. He'd done more than burgle, he'd raped and assaulted and conned folks who should know better out of their life savings. If anyone deserved to meet an early end it was this fellow.

What usually happened when no one on the force wanted to undertake this kind of investigation was that it was handed to Harry. Harry was good, he could handle delicate, messy situations, and hell, if it didn't work out and he somehow failed, why then that was one less pain in the ass.

Harry had his reservations about Keepnews, not being especially comfortable with people who were born to ten million and got it to forty, but he still couldn't help liking the man. There was something charming and boyish about him, especially when he got carried away, which he frequently did. A man with more ideas than he had money, with no time to execute them all. But above all, what Harry liked about him was his impatience, his insistence that if something were worth doing it was worth doing right at that very moment. No sense waiting around for times to get better or the conjunction of stars to improve.

In the end, partly because of Harry's testimony, Keepnews was exonerated; the D.A. decided against bringing charges of manslaughter in return for Keepnews' promise to stay out of the limelight for a while and keep his thoughts regarding the use of guns and the benefits of vigilante groups to himself. It was all a very informal agreement, but Keepnews abided by it. He was always as good as his word. It was something he prided himself on.

More than that, he made it a point never to forget those who had helped him—as well as those who had betrayed or otherwise fucked him. Harry luckily was one of those who fell into the former category.

Whenever possible, Keepnews would provide Harry with valuable information, and the kind of information he acquired was not easily obtained. You had to move in certain circles, and Harry by himself would have no way of gaining access to them. Harry got the feeling that Keepnews would like to hire him away, not for anything in particular, simply to have, like he had so many things; his house, his cars, his private jet, his yacht, his buildings in downtown San Francisco, his software company, his biological research center, and his wife. Harry figured Keepnews would stick him away in a closet somewhere, forget all about him until the occasion for his services arose, like a tuxedo you brought out for a wedding or funeral now and again. Not that it wouldn't be a real nice closet, but spending much of his life in mothballs, no matter how good the pay, was not his idea of the way he cared to spend the years that remained to him.

Keepnews was aware of Harry's feelings, and he'd stopped courting him long ago. But this was a special occasion, as he'd indicated over the phone.

He started off apologetically, saying he knew how pressed Harry was for time. "But there's no one else I can turn to, no one I can think of. Fact of the matter is I spoke to the Coast Guard and I talked to your people. Did everything proper—not because I expected satisfaction, mind you, but I wanted the record to be straight. I wanted it shown that I went through proper channels and that I got shit for my troubles, if you understand my battle plan?"

Harry understood all right, but wondered what he was leading up to.

Keepnews did not take long in coming to the point. It wasn't his nature to be evasive. He thrust forward a file full of photographs and documents pertaining to the *Hyacinth*.

"I realize you're a busy man, Harry . . ."

"You'd be surprised. I seem suddenly to find myself with a great deal of free time."

"Oh yes? How so?"

Harry didn't go into detail, but he did mention the most important part—that he was without a job for the foreseeable future.

"Well, that changes everything. I was thinking that I would work out some arrangement with you in your spare time. But seeing that your spare time isn't quite so restricted, maybe we could come to a more formal agreement. I don't want to do anything that would jeopardize your relationship with the department, of course."

Harry laughed. "Frankly, I don't see how you could jeopardize it any more than it is."

"I see your point." Keepnews rose from the Naugahyde chair and strode over to his $5000 stereo system. The speakers were unobtrusively concealed in the corners of the living room, which was a pretty good trick seeing that they were the size of dowry chests—big dowry chests. "What do you think of Monteverdi?"

"I don't have any opinion, I'm afraid."

"We have to further your education then." He placed some Monteverdi on the stereo. "The forerunner of opera," he declared.

Harry wouldn't know; Monteverdi wasn't what he did for fun, but he registered the name. No fact was without its use—eventually. "I'm surprised you didn't know about my situation, it was in the papers this morning."

"Never read the papers," Keepnews said. "San Francisco papers are shit. All papers are shit. But the San Francisco papers are especially shit. So you'll take the assignment?"

The transition was so abrupt that for a moment Harry couldn't figure what he was referring to. "About your boat you mean?"

"That's right. What do you say?"

"You haven't told me exactly what you'd like done."

"Well, check it out for one. Study the photos I just gave you, read the specifications, go down to the Marina Yacht Harbor, there's a yacht there, called *The Sojourner* now. Not a bad name even if they are pirates that took it.

34

I want you to scavenge around a little, get some good hard evidence I can use."

"Evidence that *The Sojourner* and the *Hyacinth* are one and the same?"

"Now you're talking!"

"One issue we haven't talked about."

"Money?"

"That's right."

"How'd I guess? What do you have in mind?"

Harry told him. "And funeral expenses if necessary."

"Deal. But funeral expenses?"

"Like to have all possibilities covered. But don't worry about flowers. I don't think I'd like flowers at my funeral."

"Oh no? And why is that, Harry?"

"I'm allergic to them."

Keepnews liked that and laughed heartily.

His wife heard them and came into the living room. She wanted to know what they found so humorous.

"Harry is a very funny man," Keepnews told her.

"That was the feeling I always got," said Wendy, giving Harry a conspiratorial wink he couldn't divine the meaning of.

Wendy escorted him off the grounds.

"When will we be seeing you again?"

"Depends on what I find out tonight. Could be tomorrow morning."

"That would be lovely." She was wearing a robe now over the bikini. It was easier to look at her without staring—but not much. They approached Harry's car. It needed a wash and a paint job badly. Harry kept meaning to get around to it, but there never seemed to be enough time. Until now. Just as he was about to get into it she stepped closer to him. She had that imploring expression people get on their faces when they want desperately to say something to you, but don't know just how to go about it. She struggled and at last found a way. "Did Harold tell you we're getting a divorce?"

The way she said this was so offhanded that Harry thought that he'd misheard her.

"Are you surprised?"

"Well, yes, I think I am." He gazed out at the rambling mansion up the hill. It was gleaming white in the sun, a splendid spectacle that celebrated the mating of money, architecture, and cultivated taste. Divorce was something that didn't seem to belong to a house like this; only what was beautiful and immortal should live there.

"Harold has been very nice about the whole thing. He doesn't want the divorce. We've talked about it endlessly. But we both agree it's probably the best thing."

"Mind me asking one question?"

She shrugged. "Sure, go ahead."

"Most couples, they're getting a divorce, they don't keep living together."

"We're not your usual couple. The house is big enough for the two of us. We never have to see each other if we don't want to. We haven't slept together for six months." She fixed her eyes on Harry the way an interrogator might. "Do I shock you?"

"I'm not sure shock is the right word for it. I don't know whether there's a word in the English vocabulary that's the right word for it. Maybe I'm a little old-fashioned, that could be it."

"As soon as Harold and I work things out I'll find myself a new situation."

Harry didn't know that people talked about new situations in that manner unless they were characters in the nineteenth-century novels he was compelled to read in high school.

"And how long do you think that'll be?"

"Hard to tell with this yacht thing," Wendy said. "Once everything's settled and he's got the *Hyacinth* back and the pirates put behind bars then maybe I'll move out. He's still my friend, he'll always be that, and I wouldn't want to desert him now."

"It's heartening to see there's no animosity."

36

She looked offended. "Between Harold and me? Never."

"Tell me, Wendy, what do you think is Harold's uppermost priority—getting his boat back or finding the men who killed his crew? That is, if they were killed."

It was hard to tell what she was thinking by the mysterious look on her face. Nor would she answer his question directly. All she said was, "Why do you think I want a divorce?"

Harry understood—or thought he did at any rate.

Chapter Four

That same evening, when the sky was flushed with a soft amber light that was the sun's final legacy, Harry settled down behind the wheel of his car and started down Columbus on his way to the Marina Yacht Harbor. Beside him were the documents and photos provided by Keepnews. He was not certain how he would get on board *The Sojourner* nor how he would uncover the hard evidence that would identify it absolutely as the *Hyacinth*. He would have to do what Sonny Rollins was doing to "My Old Flame" with his tenor saxophone on the radio— improvise. Sonny had his horn, Harry had his gun, but they were each only instruments; it was the mind, the imagination, that indefinable something that made it all work. Or not. It depended sometimes on the adrenalin in your blood, on the time of day or night it was. There were occasions when everything looked wrong and you couldn't see how in the world you would make it, and still it worked, held together and miraculously clicked. Of course, there were those occasions when the exact opposite happened. Dangerous occasions when it all looked perfect, then blew up in your face.

No one in the Broadway area was waiting for darkness to overtake them. Already the strip joints and the peep shows were going full-blast, pouring music and florescent colors out into the street. High-strutting hookers who you'd never catch in the light of day were parading in twos and threes, down the avenue, black and white and yellow with hair crowded thickly on their heads. Their pimps hung back in the shadows, contemplating the next several hours' profits. Youths, their minds gone blank with ludes and angel dust, roamed up and down, dazedly peering into the topless bars where the girls were bathed in harsh pink lights and compelled to writhe in simulated passion to the same jukebox tunes they'd writhed to the night before. Tourists, thinking there was some sort of new thrill to be discovered here, bore the expression of Alice in Wonderland just before she went through the looking glass.

It was only when he was close to the junction of Bay Street that he realized he was making the man in back of him angry by being in his way. A green Chevy showed up in his rearview mirror, and from what he could see there were three men in the vehicle, two in front, one in back. The driver was doing everything he could think of to pass Harry, veering into the adjacent lane, risking oncoming traffic, blasting his horn so that Harry would pull over and let him by, and, when that didn't work, he began tailgating him, drawing so close that as soon as Harry stopped for a red light, the Chevy nearly crashed into him. There was a noisy plaintive screech of tires and a further paroxysm of hornblowing.

Harry was rather amused by the frustration he was causing the joker behind him, and he had no intention of making life easier for him. On Bay Street the Chevy's driver became even more desperate; if Harry wasn't going to allow him to pass on his side then he was bound and determined to pass him on the other. What this meant was that he had to maneuver the Chevy onto the curb, half-on, half-off, in the process upsetting a couple of garbage cans which rattled noisily to the ground and terrified some unwitting pedestrians. Harry was just about to cut him off on the right—which was not difficult—when he reconsidered. For the first time he noticed in front of him—three cars ahead—a black Mercedes which was, like the Chevy, doing whatever it could to surge ahead and overcome the trap of early evening traffic. It occurred to Harry that whoever the three gentlemen in the Chevy were they had a serious interest in the gentlemen in the Mercedes. Just what that interest was was, at this point, hard to figure. So Harry decided to let the scenario go ahead without his interference—at least at this juncture. Accordingly, he got out of the way.

The blare of horns on all sides of him, growing to an earsplitting crescendo, signaled that this chase-in-progress had caught the attention of other drivers in the vicinity. They didn't like being cut off or suffering dented fenders that would draw skeptical questions from their insurance agents. But like it or not, that was just what was happening. The two cars in their fight to penetrate the traffic lurched ahead, their drivers evidently oblivious of the damage they were causing. The sickening sound of metal against metal was repeated again and again. But gradually, in recognition of the frightening resolve of these beserk people, other drivers drew out of their way, allowing them freer passage as Bay Street yielded to Marina Boulevard. Inadvertently, they paved the way for Harry who raced after them.

The men in the Mercedes and those in the Chevy were too intent on one another to pay attention to Harry. And besides, he was as anonymous as the car he drove; there was nothing to connect him to the police save his two-wave radio, which he considered using, then decided not to. All that would happen, if he alerted them, was that the drivers of the respective cars would be stopped and given summonses for speeding. And the way they were driving, accelerating with every passing block, these were not the sort of people who would find a summons for exceeding the limit by forty miles per hour a particularly humbling experience.

Better to wait, Harry thought, and find out what these people were really about. That might not be a sensible policy, but it was one that he had no compunction about adopting. On the AM station he had going Jimmy Smith was driving hard on the organ, backed by an ingenious guitarist and a drummer propelling up a harsh primal rhythm. What the number they were playing was Harry didn't know but it sure was a terrific accompaniment to the car chase in front of him.

The Mercedes shot ahead on Marina, then veered left and headed south down Presidio Drive. Traffic was lighter on this stretch, and the two cars were that much more conspicuous. The Mercedes was speeding in the direction of Golden Gate Park; the line of trees at its perimeter could be made out in the dusk.

It was not possible to tell whether the Mercedes had a destination or was simply trying to elude the Chevy. Harry, however, was beginning to get the sense that of the two possibilities the latter was the more likely.

The Mercedes was entering the park, the Chevy was gaining on it though Harry couldn't believe that it would ever catch up. But he hadn't reckoned on the driver of the Mercedes. He was apparently not equal to the car or what it could do.

The driver didn't seem to anticipate the turns he'd have to take, and at times the vehicle would stray off the paved surface, onto the grass, into clumps of bushes. Once it banged noisily into the side of an innocent oak. Could be that the driver was drunk or on drugs or else was so carried away by this enterprise that it had all gotten a bit too much for him.

Because Harry was directly behind the Chevy and because the road pursued such a twisting and unpredictable course, he was not always able to keep the Mercedes in sight. He could, however, hear it. The tires screeched maddeningly as the car bounded from one side of the road to the other. Then there was another sound—a sound of crunching shrubbery—which was followed by moments with a terrific clatter of metal yielding quickly to the unresisting surface of a boulder that jutted out nearly to the highway, a big granite thing that had been sitting for a couple of million years waiting for some excitement.

The Chevy passed right by the final resting place of the Mercedes, but only because it was going too fast to stop immediately. It slowed down with a fervent protest from the brakes and drew up to a gravelly stretch that ran flush along the road.

Harry kept going until he was hidden from view beyond a bend in the road, then stopped and got out of his car.

The Mercedes, when he crept to within sight of it, using the trees and the shadows they sent down along the high untrimmed grass to conceal himself, was a wreck. At least the front part of it was, jammed up against the boulder, practically melded into the damn thing by the force of the impact. There was nothing left of it aside from the windshield which, while resembling a roadmap with lots of roads and riverbeds, still remained intact. Where the occupants of the Mercedes had gone Harry couldn't determine. In fact, he couldn't even figure out what had happened to their pursuers. The Chevy, too, was vacant.

But he didn't have to go looking for them. They made themselves known with a sudden burst of fire. At first there were only scattered reports, then a relentless fusillade. The conflict seemed to be going on just up over the hillock and through a cluster of oaks just to Harry's left. The question he faced was whether to return to his car and alert the station or to risk getting closer to better ascertain the situation—and to do so without somehow stumbling into the middle of the fray.

He decided to return to his car. There were too many men involved for him to handle on his own. The dispatcher recognized Harry's voice immediately.

"You back with us, Inspector?" he inquired.

"Not exactly. But don't let technicalities stop you."

"Course not. I will relay the message. Ten-four."

Even from this distance the gunfire could be heard. It

was not loud enough, however, to cause the few passing cars to stop. Then again when people were shooting one another usually the best thing you could do was to keep right on going. It was only the ones like Harry who felt the pull in the opposite direction. He wasn't about to stay by his car until help arrived. By then the gunmen might all be gone. Or dead.

Harry ventured in through the oak-strewn landscape, keeping low to avoid the stray bullet that every so often tore away the bark and smaller branches from trees in Harry's immediate vicinity. As he approached the area that the gunmen had converted into a battlefield the trees grew fewer in number, allowing for an open grassy knoll. There were on the periphery of the knoll smaller boulders, cousins of the big one that had done in the Mercedes, and these were being used by the men for cover. Who was shooting at whom Harry couldn't say for sure, and which ones had come from the Mercedes and which from the Chevy was a similar mystery. Harry, however, did have one advantage; as far as he was concerned he was against both parties to the conflict, so he really didn't care who emerged victorious. His only objective here was to put a stop to the fight, though he had no idea just how he was going to go about this.

Hunkered down, he waited for the battle to define itself, for a strategy on the part of one side or the other to become evident. He was certain that this unrewarding exchange of fire couldn't go on much longer. With everyone dug in and protected as they were, no one stood a chance in hell to hit his enemy. Sooner or later someone was going to move or else they would all have to give up, go home, and think about other ways of passing a Thursday evening in San Francisco.

In his assessment of the situation, Harry proved correct, though this did not necessarily mean anyone would give him any awards for the accuracy of his judgment. When it came to awards, people seemed more interested in taking them away from him.

In any case, someone moved, then someone else joined

42

him. They didn't risk exposing themselves on the knoll. There were better and less painful ways of committing suicide, after all. Instead they clung to the darkness that was especially friendly on the perimeter of the knoll; there there were the trees and the brambles and brush. Their opponents apparently had failed to see them because they were still aiming in the same general direction as before. One of the men had stayed behind, maintaining an even level of fire so as to give his friends more time in which to skirt around the knoll and spring their little surprise.

Harry couldn't resist spoiling their fun. It was simply too much of a temptation. He was the wild card in the deck, the X part of the equation. Since he had the two men in view—and the view was growing better all the time since they kept coming closer, having no idea that Harry was monitoring their progress—he decided to wait no longer. He raised his Magnum and fired—but not to hit either of them. That wasn't his purpose.

Astonished, even a bit incredulous, the two gunmen jumped back, firing wildly since they couldn't understand where this unexpected assault had originated. Harry fired again. And now, alerted to the two men's presence, their enemies on the opposite end of the knoll began firing in their direction too. Someone's aim was good or else he was just lucky. The man who was hit probably wouldn't spend much time contemplating which it was; the blood was pumping out of his lower back too fast for him to pay much attention to anything else. He lay in a bed of green detritus, but wouldn't stay still. Instead he thrashed about, screaming words that got drowned out by the increasing fury of the bullets flying every which way over the knoll.

The second man apparently managed to get himself to shelter before he was hit. His flight seemed to encourage the assailants across the knoll because now one of their number emerged, testing the atmosphere, maybe in preparation for a full-scale assault. Could be these jokers were playing at World War II? Harry thought. Summer nights can get boring around town.

Harry set out with the intention of circling around the knoll, laying down a barrage that wasn't meant to hit anyone but rather to confuse them. And confuse them it did. They fired at Harry, they fired at each other, they went through one clip after another, trying like hell to achieve something significant for all their trouble.

Way in the distance, sounding more like cows bellowing than anything else, you could make out the sirens of the squad cars. High time help arrived, Harry thought. But help was a mixed blessing. The appearance of the police might panic these gun-wielding gentlemen and result in considerably more bloodshed. Not that Harry cared about these characters, but he feared for the lives of the men he served with—or used to serve with before a D.A. named Nolan began reciting Supreme Court decisions to him.

It seemed to him that he was at a point midway between the two groups of gunmen. But for the moment he had no way of knowing since the fire had subsided, maybe because they wanted to be absolutely certain it was sirens they were hearing. But the imminent coming of the police evidently didn't quite put the fear of God into them because in half a minute they resumed, though their bullets were doing little more than scooping up dirt and thudding into tree trunks.

Then one of the men downrange from Harry allowed his head to appear above the craggy rock formation behind which he'd been hiding; he was obviously inspecting the territory, looking for a way out. The sirens were growing louder. The police were a factor to take into consideration right about this time.

Harry risked breaking his own cover, possessed by a compulsion to put a stop to this man's flight. He had a sudden vision of himself standing in the middle of the knoll explaining to his colleagues just what had happened and where in hell everyone had gone to and why he couldn't save one for questioning—because he suspected that the man flattened out in the dirt back there had long since given up any notion of surviving.

The man Harry had elected to take in saw him, couldn't help but see him with the noise he was producing. Not much noise maybe but enough—crackling twigs underfoot, scraping past bushes that refused to let anyone go by without announcing their passage—but there was nothing Harry could do about it, not if he wanted to maintain his speed.

The man and a friend of his who'd secreted himself among the fossilized crevices of the rock directed their fire at Harry, assuming he was leading some kind of attack. Their shots made the going treacherous but Harry, by zigzagging and dodging, escaped them, sustaining only rough scratches from the brambles and thorns that assaulted him in the dark, scraping skin from his face and hands.

Across the knoll, surprised and probably incredibly confused by this unexpected onslaught, the opposition opened fire—not at Harry but at the rock formation. The men they were targeting were now so preoccupied with bringing down Harry they had thrown caution to the wind.

One of the two shooting at Harry cried out. He then cried out again as if to reaffirm his pain. A .38 had caught him in the side of the face, gone right through one cheek, clipping off a good bit of bridgework, then gone out the other, leaving this great big bloody hole through which even the slight steady breeze off the bay could whistle. Though the wound was ugly it wasn't lethal, but that did not make any difference to the gunman insofar as the pain was concerned. He dropped his weapon and pressed both hands to his injuries. His friend had to go it alone.

The friend did not much like proceeding with the solo act since his only intention had been to escape from the field in the first place. But with gunfire plaguing him from across the knoll and now with Harry diving onto a steeply angled moss-covered rock, threatening with his Magnum, escape was out of the question.

Harry, taking advantage of his distraction, gained

ground, flattened himself out, then rushed him again. The rounds he got off forced his target to lower himself back into his Ice Age souvenir. "Shut the fuck up," Harry could hear him urging his bleeding friend who was able to release just a sad whimper, a sob caught perpetually in the throat. A sound like that could set a man on edge.

At last the poor trapped bastard couldn't take it any longer. He decided he might as well chance crawling out of his lair in hope nobody would notice or noticing, give a damn.

But as he did so, two rounds—neither of them Harry's because Harry wasn't in any position to hit him—struck him from the side. One was supposed to. It broke a few ribs in its journey, then got stuck somewhere in the right lung. The other had ricocheted up from a stone and caught him in the groin. You couldn't say that one killed him and the other didn't; he might have lived with just one of the injuries, but they had acted in concert and sucked the life right out of him. It seemed like going through a lot of trouble to die.

From the trees across the knoll flashlight beams shone, prying apart the darkness, separating the shadows of vegetation from the shadows of men with guns. Dogs barked furiously, enraged at having been dragged from the comfort of their kennels for this sort of outing where people were as liable to shoot them as their masters. And shoot they did, disregarding warnings that it was the police they were dealing with now and not just another bunch of hoodlums looking for new ways to die.

Harry found himself, uncharacteristically, isolated from the action. Didn't like it one bit. Leaving the cheekless man where he was, sponging up the copious flow of blood with hands caked by dirt, Harry scrambled across the knoll. It wasn't completely safe—bullets that hadn't found a home yet had a tendency to puncture holes in the grassy stretch of land—but no one was firing at Harry. No one seemed to remember him or realize he was there.

Harry got a rhythm going; the energy that propelled

him could have gotten a funeral limousine through the Indianopolis 500 in record time, and he had within the span of a minute gotten across the open space. But even so the battle, between the surviving gunmen and the police, seemed to be drifting away from him. He couldn't quite close in on it.

For a few moments everything was chaos—dogs were howling and men were shouting orders and abusing God, mother, and country. Flashlights went on and off in a weird progression. At intervals Harry thought he could see what was happening, only to have the visual blotted out completely, leaving behind a confused audio of hoarse voices and gun reports.

When the lights fell his way Harry sometimes caught a glimpse of a man or rather a shadow that looked and moved like a man. Harry held his fire, not wishing to shoot one of his own men. That was the last thing he needed to do, given how precarious his situation was already down at headquarters.

From deep within the cluster of trees to his right came a booming voice, amplified by a bullhorn: "This is the San Francisco Police Department. We order you to throw down your weapons and give yourselves up." Despite the authority invested in the command, the only response was a noisy burst of fire.

Now the man Harry'd seen before was thrown in sharp relief by a flashlight beam. To escape the incriminating light he raced downhill, panicking before a hail of bullets could catch up with him.

He had a mistaken idea of where safety lay.

"That's it right there," Harry called to him, his Magnum ready to tear a hole through the man's chest.

The man wanted to stop, but the momentum of his flight prevented him. He finally skittered to a halt, casting aside his gun and raising his hands in surrender. He was a smart fellow, Harry thought, to recognize when the odds no longer favored him.

Up close, the gunman looked like an overworked bank teller. He could have used a bit more sun. There was no

47

fear on his face though, only deep disgruntlement that things should have worked out this way.

There were a few more gunshots, then nothing, just the cicadas who obviously weren't about to let human beings upset their nightly songfest.

A number of uniformed men sprang into view, their faces still hidden in shadows so that Harry couldn't yet distinguish one from another. Gradually they were close enough for Harry to identify them. They advanced cautiously, fearful that the danger wasn't over.

Bob Togan, a sergeant who'd traded vice for this sort of circus, took one look at Harry and shook his head. "You," he said simply. It wasn't that he had expected Harry—the dispatcher hadn't mentioned Harry's name in the report—it was just that somehow seeing Harry didn't really surprise him. Harry had this odd habit of turning up in odd places. Places where there was likely to be a good deal of blood in the vicinity.

"That's right. How are you doing, Bob?"

"Well as can be expected." He gave the prisoner a derisory glance. "You read him his rights?"

"I'm not exactly on the force now."

"Oh no? Could have had me fooled." Togan knew very well what was happening with Harry; he just enjoyed feigning ignorance. The prisoner meanwhile was looking from one man to the other, confused over this exchange.

Across the knoll a couple of officers were inspecting the damage around the rock formation. The cicadas were experiencing some competition now from ambulance sirens, which made a mockery of the pleasant quiet you expect from a park at night.

Togan ordered the prisoner led off. He wanted him out of his sight quickly. "You have any idea what this was all about, Harry?"

"Can't say as I do."

"Some help you are. Where are you going?"

"I got an appointment to keep."

"Oh yeah, what does she look like? You can't always be doing this sort of shit, not all the time."

Harry ignored him. "One thing, Bob. When you file your report I wish you'd neglect to mention my name."

Togan laughed. "Hey, what's wrong, don't want the glory that's coming to you?"

"You know what you can do with your glory, Bob."

"I got an idea." He was still laughing. Harry was merging with the dark; that's one thing Harry did terrifically, fading out of sight so you'd never know he was there to begin with.

Chapter Five

Bill Evans was on the radio now; a lulling ballad for lovers you'll never see again. The music was soothing after the sound and light show in Golden Gate Park. Something like a headache was at work in Harry's skull, a dull throb that hadn't decided whether it wanted to become a full-fledged headache or fade away entirely.

Bill Evans gave way to a news commentator with a voice that went well with a final beer at the end of the night. Only it wasn't the end of the night. It was, in fact, just shy of ten o'clock. The events of the last hour had sufficiently drained Harry so that he considered putting off his visit to the *Hyacinth* or *The Sojourner* or whatever the hell they were calling it tonight. He had an idea of taking in a movie or else of going to bed. But he knew very well that he would find his way to the hijacked yacht—that is if Keepnews was correct in surmising that it was hijacked. Harry had this thing about obligation; it was his personal code. It didn't much coincide with the way the department thought about how people should behave. Actually, it didn't much coincide with the way his friends thought either, which may have explained why he had very few friends. But whether they were friends or enemies they held the same opinion when it came to

49

Harry: one day his sense of obligation was going to kill him.

As he drove back toward the marina he was subjected to no further distractions such as the one that had gotten him off on the road into Golden Gate Park. Had there been any he might have foregone the temptation and continued on anyway; he'd had enough for one night.

And that may have explained why he failed to notice he was being followed. There was someone way in back of him in a BMW; it had a clean cocoa color to it and was not the kind of vehicle people ordinarily employ for the purposes of tailing a person.

But it didn't matter. The BMW was way in back of Harry, proceeding at a very leisurely speed. Harry was in no hurry, neither was the tail.

Harry parked his car a couple of blocks from the marina. He wanted to walk. He also didn't wish to make his interest in the marina known without doing some preliminary reconnaissance. All the documents and photographs relating to the structure and design of the craft in question were hidden under the car seat. Harry didn't need them anymore, the significant particulars were in his throbbing head.

The BMW pulled up about a block farther from where Harry had parked. Its occupant—and there was only one occupant—waited for a couple of minutes before getting out and having a look around.

Like a restless nighttime stroller, Harry wandered past the marina, casually observing the yachts on the other side of the fence. In the lights that demarcated the mooring slips he could make out the flybridge of one boat, the pilothouse of another, the empty masts of another. In the dark water that lapped against their hulls the reflections of these boats shimmered magically.

But what struck Harry as odd was that there was no sign of life, none on the boats, none on the docks. There should be some security presence here, he thought, at least a bored watchman doing the rounds. But if he was anywhere nearby he wasn't bothering to make himself known. Maybe nodded out somewhere, dreaming dreams of the big bucks that could make boats like these happen.

But where among them was the rechristened *Hyacinth?* From the outside he couldn't tell. No way to identify these yachts at this distance. He decided he would have to climb over for a better look. He located a portion of the fence that was unexposed by light and maneuvered himself up and over with little difficulty. Didn't make much noise doing this, but when he was down he looked sharply in all directions, prepared to confront someone who would want to know why he'd chosen to enter the marina in such an unorthodox fashion. But if anyone had noticed Harry he wasn't troubling himself to step out and talk to him.

All Harry could hear was water lapping the hulls and the rumble of cars passing back and forth on Marina Boulevard. Once or twice he thought he heard the docks creak, but if that's what they were doing it was on their own volition. No human feet were causing those sounds. No human feet, no human anything.

Harry proceeded farther, drawing closer to the yachts, comparing each one of them to the picture he carried in his head. The cutter he was seeking was not such a unique model that it would easily stand out among the others. But there were certain idiosyncrasies that he'd been instructed by Keepnews to look for. And presumably there was only one boat with the name *The Sojourner* spelled out on its bow.

It took him a while, but he found it. Whatever its name, it was a beautiful specimen all right. The *Hyacinth* had been painted white with a trimming on its decks that bore the color of its name. But it wasn't white any longer. Instead it was a dark blue, the color of sky just before it fades to night. The trimming was submerged under the blue as well. So, Harry thought, probably was the blood.

He stared at the boat for a minute, maybe a bit longer, not sure exactly what he was going to do. In truth, he hadn't really thought about just how he would obtain the proof Keepnews wanted. He figured it would come to him once he got here: this is called the art of the improviser. But for this short interval his mind was a blank. He seemed to be in neutral. Goddamn motor needs cranking up again, Harry concluded, then went about the business of clambering on board.

With a pocketknife, one of those intricate items of Swiss manufacture equipped with can opener and toothpick, Harry stooped down and began to run the blade along the surface of the deck. One lone light atop the pilothouse provided the only available illumination, but Harry was not exposed by it. In an atmosphere of nearly total silence the scraping blade as it fought against metal sounded much too loud. At intervals Harry would stop and listen closely, but he could only hear the bay water eddying about the boats. His efforts at digging up paint off the deck proved futile. He turned his attention to the railing that ran alongside the stern, probing it with the knife to see if any paint came off.

He was immediately rewarded. Chips of blue flew off as soon as he sank the blade in. Only two coats at most had been applied; what lay beneath was another color, which Harry couldn't make out with certainty because of the dimness. But he was reasonably sure that it would be purplish in hue—hyacinth.

That might or might not constitute definitive proof. In any case, he wanted to see more. He decided to go below deck. The door to the cabin offered little resistance when he tugged at it; the boat's most recent owners had been careless about securing it. Darkness greeted him, and a series of steps was barely discernible. Though Harry's hand found a toggle switch on the wall to his right, one which would probably give him light to see by, he resisted using it. The last thing he needed was to attract unnecessary attention if there were a guard patrolling the slips.

Carefully, to keep from tripping and tumbling into the murk, Harry proceeded down the steps. When he reached bottom his shoes became partially submerged in a soft carpet. He advanced another few paces and promptly bumped into something sharp that caused him to wince

52

and mutter a curse against inanimate objects. Turned out it was a table with metal corners that could prove lethal. God knows what else awaited him in his reconnaissance, but sooner or later he was going to have to risk a light. Otherwise this whole expedition would be futile.

Now the substance underfoot changed consistency. No longer was it carpet, rather it was dirt, sod. Something leafy brushed against his face, something else with nettles attached raked his arms. For all he knew he could be back in Golden Gate Park again. What the hell was he doing amidst this vegetation? Keepnews, he recalled, liked rare tropical plants and gardening, but he hadn't told Harry to expect a small jungle—must have slipped his mind.

Harry drew back, finding surer footing on the carpet again. He turned and moved in the other direction, his arms in front of him to give him a sense of what came next. There was, on his left side, a long narrow couch with lots of cushions stacked on it. He kept going and plowed right into something hard. "Shit," he said pronouncing judgment on this exploration.

What he'd come up against was a bulkhead. Directly below it was a passageway intended for people who needed another four inches or so before they reached Harry's height. Kneading his bruised forehead, he stooped and made his way through the passageway. He now found himself in the kitchen. There was a small oval window here. It looked out upon the Pacific, not the docks. If a light was possible any place it would be here. All he had to do was find it. After some substantial groping he located the switch. A lamp above the counter eagerly responded, bathing the area in a warm, faintly amber light.

This was sufficient for him to see into the rest of the cabin beyond the passageway. The table was much larger than he'd imagined, the artificial garden, situated midway across the room, much smaller.

He began methodically to open up everything there was to be opened, cabinets, bulkheads, drawers, not certain of

53

exactly what he expected to find but expecting to find something.

What he found, at first, was the sort of paraphernalia he'd have figured a boat like this would be stocked with: utensils, heaters, life preservers, blankets, a weather chart recorder, cans of biochemical gel, a digital depth sounder, a refrigerator cluttered with beer and champagne, tins of coffee. But nothing that could convince a judge that all these things had once belonged to Keepnews. You could fingerprint them of course, but you'd need a warrant simply to get onto the boat. And a warrant would require grounds for reasonable suspicion. Keepnews didn't have those grounds. Harry had yet to find them.

He abandoned the kitchen, then the cabin because they refused to yield anything useful. He did, however, discover another passageway he hadn't seen before. This led to what seemed to be a utility area. Here he also lacked more than a trickle of light and ended up stepping on something rubber. It was a dinghy with webbing for seats, with both hand and foot pumps to inflate the thing. What it was doing smack in the middle of the floor Harry couldn't imagine. It seemed careless to have left it here. Then it came to him. When his foot had inadvertently pressed down on it, the dinghy hadn't responded the way a hollow rubber object ordinarily would have. Too hard.

Snapping open his knife, he dug the tip of it into the dinghy. There was a slight hiss of air but nothing else. The knife was meeting resistance. It wasn't air that the rubber tubing contained.

Applying greater pressure to the knife, he worked a fairly extensive hole into the dinghy, worrying it until he could get his hands into it. He caught hold of something, pulled it out. It wasn't necessary to look for better lighting to determine what it was. Harry knew by the feel of it alone. It was a glassine envelope, presumably one of many thousands tucked within the dinghy. Nothing in it, however: no heroin.

It was possible, Harry considered, that elsewhere in the dinghy the heroin itself might be found. Or possibly it was hidden in another crevice of the yacht, awaiting unloading. Harry assumed though that it had been carted off before, maybe as early as the first night in port. But there was always the chance that the hijackers had not found their opportunity and that the drug was still on board. Harry could not resist the temptation to look farther.

No longer so scrupulous about perforating the dinghy he set about gouging great tears in it, but all he revealed were more glassine envelopes. He was about to give up on the dinghy and see what other peculiar treasures this utility area had to offer when he heard a noise behind him. Not much of a noise—an asthmatic's muffled wheeze would have been more obtrusive. But still it alerted him. His gaze shifted to the side. His ears were cocked, acutely sensitive now. The noise was not repeated.

All at once Harry felt trapped, for there was no exit from the utility area except the way he'd come in. The air was too warm, too dense and stale. He rose, deciding to forgo further exploration for the time being. Sliding a glassine envelope into his pocket, he began down the passageway, his Magnum in hand.

The interior of the cabin was as quiet as before. In the poor light streaming through the passageway from the kitchen nothing unusual presented itself. Harry wasn't comforted. He felt that he was no longer alone, that his movements were being watched. But there was no visual cue to corroborate this sensation.

Just as he started up the steps he heard another noise. This one was louder and more penetrating than the last. The noise coincided with a vast amount of pain that sprang up suddenly from the base of his neck and in an instant monopolized every nerve fiber his head possessed. Only before his consciousness vanished completely did he identify the noise. It was the sound of a club slamming against his skull.

Chapter Six

Two men stood over him. One had just emerged from the garden Keepnews had built to remind him what green looked like while he plied the seas in search of tuna. The other was positioned on the steps, having come down just in time to see Harry collapse. He didn't look comfortable, sprawled out there on the floor. But it didn't particularly matter.

The man who'd clubbed him raised his eyes to his companion, watching him with indifference as he considered the range and cocked his Smith and Wesson, prepared to obliterate Harry's head.

"Wouldn't do that," the first man said as though this was an afterthought, not an important issue but one worth thinking about for a couple of seconds.

"Oh, why not?" It was so tempting a target. The man with the Smith and Wesson liked seeing solid things turn to bloody pulp. Heads especially.

"He's going to be dead any which way. Looks better if he drowned, banged his head against something and drowned. A bullet hole, you can't say he drowned. Why leave behind a lead if you can help it?"

"Oh, you're some kind of an Einstein, I can see that much, Milano."

The man named Milano shrugged. "I been in this business longer than you. Put the gun away. We got to blow this mother. Fish are getting impatient."

The fish needn't have been too impatient. The good ship *Hyacinth*-turned-*The Sojourner* was about to take its last journey—straight down to the bottom of San Francisco Bay.

Small explosives were all that were necessary, nothing extravagant, and they were conveniently already in place,

56

strategically implanted in the diesel motors, in the aft cockpit bulkhead, in the pulpit where the two anchors were cached in the Moorings' case. The holes that the three simultaneous detonations would produce would ensure a hasty demise for the luxury yacht.

"I don't see what fuckin' difference it would make," said the man, who with great reluctance consented to put his weapon away.

"It makes a difference," Milano said. "Take my word for it, it makes a difference."

The drug had been offloaded. There was no use left for the boat, especially now that its true purpose had been uncovered. The two men scrambled up the stairs and were soon over the side and running fast along the docks. As soon as they reached the perimeter of the marina area a radio transmitter activated the explosives. They could scarcely be heard, just muffled roars. Within a few moments pale gray smoke rose into the air, but there wasn't much of it and it soon faded from view.

At first the yacht didn't seem to want to do anything. It sat where it was, contentedly, but then it listed to the right, banging against the side of the dock. Gradually the waterline rose until it was flush with the edge of the deck. Another minute or so and it would disappear beneath the bay.

It was the water trickling along the rug that Harry felt first. Not a lot of water. A leaky faucet would have produced more. And in any case Harry didn't feel much like responding, water or no water. He was not completely out. But he didn't think he'd particularly object to a condition of unconsciousness—a painless welcoming darkness rather appealed to him. Lights, crazy colored lights, spun around in his mind, red, blue, yellow, the primary colors; and each color seemed to be accompanied by its own brand of pain—this one sharp, this one sharper still, this one throbbing.

It wasn't a trickle any longer. The water was gathering quantity and force; there could be no doubt about it even in Harry's dazed mind, it was coming in quicker, washing his legs, cresting about his torso and his arms, and even though his head was turned to the side, it was threatening his ability to breathe. Almost involuntarily, he twisted his head farther toward the ceiling, attempting to keep water from infiltrating his mouth and nasal cavities. But all such contortions did him no good. The water was accumulating too fast, and it would soon engulf him.

A part of Harry's mind, the oldest part, full of instincts and primitive urgings, forced him to act. Groaning, he extended himself, picking his head up out of the gathering water, though the pain shot through his whole body in protest. Couldn't worry about that now, he thought hazily, must do something about this goddamn water.

Only at this point did it reach him that what he was smelling was salt. It was seawater that was pouring into the cabin. Though he had no idea where it was all coming from, and not the slightest inclination to find out, he realized that this meant the boat was sinking. Hardly delighted at the prospect of going down with it, he summoned all the energy that was left to him and did something that vaguely resembled a pushup; this maneuver succeeded in getting him just above the water. From this position he extended one, then the other arm, hoping he would not slip and lose his balance—because he really didn't know whether he could go through this painful process of getting up again.

Half-climbing, half-crawling, he managed to get to the top of the steps that ascended to the deck. The water was pursuing him, attacking the steps and leaving only a foot and a half below the ceiling of the cabin that was not flooded. What made all this worse was that there was no light, just pitch darkness permeated by the pungent smell of salt water and the sound of the bay breaking through the fragile walls of the ill-fated *Hyacinth*.

Gasping for air, coughing with the water he'd already inhaled, Harry reached the handle of the door and pulled.

Nothing happened. The door wasn't budging. Could be the men who'd bludgeoned him had locked it just to ensure the certainty of his death. The water was nearly to shoulder level now, allowing him little room to maneuver and scarcely any purchase at all. He pulled again, struggling to maintain his hold on the handle which was growing increasingly slippery not only with the water but with his sweat. When it seemed that nothing was going to work he drove his body against it, hoping to batter it down.

Just then the whole boat tilted, sagging way over to the right. With this sudden jolting motion everything turned practically upsidedown. Harry was no longer ramming the door, he was falling on it. Water swirled around him, getting into his mouth and nose and eyes so that he couldn't see at all, though with it so goddamn dark there wasn't anything to see to begin with. He fought to get his head above water, which was not always possible.

Still, there were pockets of air here and there and when he found one he took full advantage of it. Responding to the pressure of Harry's body and the massive weight of all the water that had collected on it, the door to the cabin yielded, and Harry found himself propelled right through the opening.

But he wasn't free. Water only gave way to more water. The boat was almost completely sunk; only the roof of the pilot house and the tops of the masts remained visible. The rest of the *Hyacinth* was taking its last voyage and gaining speed with every additional foot it descended.

Harry wasn't in a particular mood to go swimming, but that was the only choice available to him. But the problem now was that he had no idea where he was, whether on the deck or above it, the world was just wet and black, with a great many obstacles: all he could do was keep trying to head in an upward direction, though what was up and what was down was hard to distinguish.

He couldn't breathe lest he take in more water, and he

59

couldn't not breathe because his lungs were demanding oxygen and with every passing second threatened to burst with the pain.

He thought he discerned a light but it was very far away and even as he made for it he had no idea whether he was hallucinating or not. It just was the only thing to aim for, this blurry luminous speck obscured by the murky green substance of water. By concentrating on the light, Harry managed to put a distance between himself and the pain he felt. Not much of a distance but enough for him to make some headway against the water.

Now there was a groan. It came from the complicated machinery that held the *Hyacinth* together; it was a dying chant. The boat was fully under. It might have been the way the current was moving, but whatever it was, the *Hyacinth* keeled sharply to the left, in the opposite direction from where it had been listing before. One of the masts came down on Harry. It didn't hit him head-on, rather it grazed him, catching him on his left leg. Though the injury to his leg was slight, the blow slowed Harry's momentum and forced him off course. He lost the light and had no sense of where to look for it again. Not that it mattered; he hadn't the strength left to do anything about it even if the light should magically reappear. The pain in his body was so immense that it didn't seem reasonable to fight it anymore. His straining lungs could not continue to endure the agony he was subjecting them to.

This is some fucking way to go, he thought, waiting in vain for his life to pass before his eyes, the way it was supposed to when you were drowning. But it didn't happen. Neither his life nor anyone else's showed up. Just my luck, he considered distantly, just my goddamn luck to be deprived of a last-minute show.

Then he let go and the darkness opened up.

Chapter Seven

It was just that the darkness didn't want to keep him very long. When he opened his eyes Harry found himself stretched out on moist wooden planks. There were lights and a sky cluttered with stars, and there were people who seemed to be looming over him and so far as he knew these were not the sorts of things you associated with heaven or hell. Particularly not hell. They weren't going to provide you with a glimpse of stars and sky in hell.

"Harry? Harry? You alive?"

The question seemed not at all irrelevant or gratuitous. Harry thought in fact that it was a highly crucial inquiry, and he wasn't so sure he had the correct response down yet. There was so much pain at work in his abused body that the very notion of trying to say something defeated him. Couldn't do it. Didn't even care to keep his eyes open, could barely make out anything anyway.

"He's alive," someone else said. "He has a pulse, he just opened his eyes, that's more than a lot of folks do."

"Yeah, well, he might not stay alive if we don't get him some medical attention soon."

"You don't know Harry. That son of a bitch doesn't know how to die. No one ever taught him."

Very hazily Harry's mind registered what was going on around him. He just wasn't interested in reacting to it. They were hoisting his body up off the dock and onto a stretcher, and they were doing this real gently, afraid maybe that some important part of his anatomy might drop out on them. Someone was busy giving his arm an injection, adding the pain of a needle prick to all the other pain he'd amassed in the last half hour or so.

61

Then his rescuers—he presumed they were his rescuers —proceeded with him down the length of the dock. They stopped suddenly.

"Who you got there?"

Harry recognized the voice but he couldn't remember to whom it belonged.

"Friend of yours."

"Oh yeah?" A pause while he took a look. "Oh shit. Harry again! What the fuck's he doing here?"

"How should I know what he's doing here? He washed up with the kelp. Seems he was on a boat. Boat went one way, he didn't want to follow."

"First he's running around loose in Golden Gate Park, then he's fucking with sinking yachts in a marina. What is it with this guy? Would you get him out of my sight?"

Had his lungs been up to it, Harry would have laughed in spite of the pain. He knew whose voice it was now. Sergeant Bob Togan's.

When he came back to some semblance of life twenty-eight hours later, Harry discovered that his mind was more or less in place. The problem was he couldn't hold it there. It had this tendency to stray, and he'd find himself staring blankly out into space, wondering where he was.

He was in a hospital room. A semi-private. The man who shared the room was hidden from Harry by an opaque curtain that divided the space in half. But Harry sensed from the strained wheezing noises the man was producing he couldn't be in very good shape. He didn't think he ever wanted to see who it was.

Fluids raced into him from one tube connected to a bottle above him and ran out of him from another connected to a bottle beyond his line of sight. The pain wasn't so bad now, it had eased into something tolerable, and it was possible that one day not so far in the future it would all go away. Feeling his face with hands raw and scraped he found that he'd developed a harsh stubble. He imagined how he looked and decided he didn't care to look into a mirror in the foreseeable future.

He tried not to think. When he thought, the pain came back to him. No memory was completely painless maybe, but this was ridiculous.

What puzzled him most were the flowers, bright, beautiful, exotic, springing up from a porcelain vase. Somebody had gone to a lot of trouble for him. He couldn't imagine who it could be.

If there was a knock on the door, he didn't hear it. Too preoccupied by the wheezing in the next bed. It was Bob Togan, holding a package in his hand.

"They told me you're back among the living, Harry," he said, pulling a seat up to the bed. He glanced around at the room. "Who sent you the flowers?"

"Don't know. The note didn't say."

"Anonymous admirer. Everybody needs at least one of them." He was not here on a friendly visit Harry knew. He wanted useful information. Harry was not certain how much of that he had to give him.

"What can I do for you, Bob?"

Togan shrugged. "How about telling me what you were doing out on that boat for a start?"

"I was doing some research for a friend. Private business."

"Private?" Togan's brow crinkled in perplexity.

"You forget I'm not on the force these days."

"I didn't forget." He hesitated, he didn't like grilling another cop, particularly one who held a rank higher than his—even though Harry was on suspension. "Are you going to make this hard for me?"

Harry had just lapsed, his mind was drifting. He had to ask Togan to repeat what he said. Togan didn't. Instead he asked Harry if he was acquainted with the sunken yacht's owner. Harry admitted he was.

"So Keepnews sent you?"

"You'll have to live with the conclusions you jump to, Bob."

"You see who the fuckers were that did that to you?" He indicated the bandage that was curled around the back of Harry's head.

"They're better than that. Didn't see shit."

"Figured as much."

"And I expect you have no idea who they are."

"None as to their identities. But we have some kind of clue given the nature of their business."

"Ah yes, their business."

"Too bad the smack didn't go down with the ship, but with the haul they must have had on board, hey, that'll buy a hundred yachts."

"You should have gotten there sooner. Like a couple of days sooner."

"Haines was working on it. It was under investigation."

"Haines," Harry muttered.

"What can I tell you, Harry? You know how much shit comes in here all the time. The fucking Coast Guard should be doing this sort of thing, but you know, nobody's got the budget, nobody's got the manpower, everyone passes the buck. Look, you're alive, that's something."

"I suppose I should take this opportunity to express my gratitude for fishing me out."

"Don't express it to me. We weren't the ones to fish you out. We found you lying on the dock when we got to the marina. Somebody had already done the fishing for us."

Harry looked closely at Togan, scrutinizing him to see if maybe he was joking. But it was no joke. "So who was it then?"

"Beats me. Maybe the same person who called us up and alerted us in the first place."

"No record of who called in?"

"Anonymous informant if you want to get technical, that's all I can tell you."

Harry didn't say anything for several moments, reflecting on this, puzzling out who it could be. He directed his gaze to the flowers. This was one hell of a secret admirer, he thought.

"I thought you might like to know we did some backgrounders on those bastards we caught at Golden Gate."

Harry had completely forgotten about them and the incident that had led to their capture. It seemed to him that it had all happened years ago.

"What did you find?"

"They're all involved in drugs. Smack mostly, some coke and angel dust when the urge strikes them, but their bread and butter is brown Mexican shit."

"Oh, so what's the problem that they started blowing each other away?"

"The problem is they belong to rival syndicates. Apparently someone's moved too much shit in all at once, and you know how these things work, everyone wants a piece of the action. It's too big for the locals to handle. You just happened into the middle of the war is all."

"I wouldn't be mistaken in thinking that you've made the same connection I have," Harry said.

"No, you wouldn't be mistaken. No telling how much Mexican was unloaded from the good ship *The Sojourner. . . .*"

"*Hyacinth,*" Harry corrected him.

"By any name. That's Haines' department. But my point is the market's gotten flooded. It creates havoc among our favorite local pushers."

"How about Father Nick? He's in a position to cause a lot of havoc."

"Father Nick." Togan didn't want to think about Father Nick after the furor Harry had provoked by arresting him. "If you're smart, Harry, you'll want to stay far away from Father Nick."

Harry spread out his hands as though to embrace his cheerless little hospital room. "How much farther away can I get than this?"

"You got a point." Togan rose from his chair. "But just in case, the boys down at the department, as an expression of our concern and—"

"You going to cut the bullshit?"

"Eventually." Togan seemed a bit nervous about making this presentation. He held out the package he'd come in with. "Well, here it is. We figure the way you're going you'll be needing it."

By the shape of the package Harry had a good idea what it would be. Still, he pretended surprise when on opening it he revealed a gleaming .44 Magnum. Unquestionably, it was something he could use since his last .44 was down at the bottom of San Francisco Bay.

"I appreciate this."

"We're always thinking of you, Harry." Togan neglected to say what direction their thoughts took. As he stepped to the door he turned abruptly to ask Harry how much longer he was obliged to stay confined in the hospital.

"They don't say. Doctors are like cops, they look at you, nod gravely, and walk away. You don't know what's on their minds. But my feeling is I won't be here long."

"Later then. And if by chance you should remember what you were doing down at that boat feel free."

"Absolutely, Bob, absolutely."

Togan hadn't been gone for more than five minutes when Harry disconnected the catheters they'd wired him with. Wasn't hard, a little excess blood quickly staunched, and he was free. Climbing out of bed was another matter. A child of three had more dexterity than Harry at this point. He used his hands to prop himself up. As soon as he attained a fully vertical position it was all he could do to remain there. His head felt woozy as though he'd been drinking for the last twenty-four hours and had just now registered its impact. But he was bound and determined to get out of this place. Like jail cells, hospital rooms were places for other men—and women. Including whoever occupied the next bed.

Nobody would ever die on the Keepnews estate. Too beautiful a place for it. Too much green, too many flowers, too much water flowing through irrigation ducts and out of stone fountains fashioned into nymphs and

66

satyrs. When the time came for people like Keep-news they would go down into the city for their sendoff.

Harry wasn't sure how he felt. He'd been out of the hospital for all of three and a half hours. It was as if the headache he'd begun his little adventure with had spread into the rest of his body, providing a constant dull ache that slowed him down but couldn't quite stop him.

Wendy wasn't around to welcome him this time. Instead a man of considerable size and untrusting eyes appeared. He wore a plain, checkered shirt and dungarees no designer would have gone near. He could have been one of the gardeners or else a security guard. Maybe both.

"Mr. Keepnews expecting you?"

"Mr. Keepnews is always expecting me. It's just I don't always turn up on time."

The man noddod, not sure how to take this. "You'll wait a minute," he said. It was not a question. "What's your name?"

Harry told him. This seemed to ring a bell. "Then I suppose it's all right if you head on up. You know the way?"

Harry knew the way. You could see it from his vantage point: the slow gracious curve of the gravel road up to the house.

Keepnews must have spotted him from one of his picture windows. He came out to greet him. A frown was on his face. "Harry," he started, "you shouldn't be here. You should be in bed. I just got back from the hospital, no one knows what happened to you. The nurses are frantic."

"It's nice to know you're missed."

Harry got out of his car and walked with a purposeful stride toward the millionaire. Walking was like a whole new enterprise for him, but he was getting the hang of it.

Keepnews, despite his expression of concern, admired

67

Harry's precipitous flight from his hospital bed. Under the circumstances he would have done the same thing.

Keepnews brought Harry out to the verandah in back, which, with its inlaid mosaic floor and marble portico, resembled an old Venetian piazza more than anything else. He insisted that Harry have a drink although he himself refrained.

Then he placed himself in a big wicker chair and leaning forward indicated that Harry should tell him everything he had learned.

Harry tried to, but kept getting vaguely distracted by the music that was filtering down from one of the open upstairs windows. It wasn't Monteverdi, being too percussive and rambunctious; more likely it was Wendy's music than her husband's.

"So you found no heroin?"

"I suspect it had already been removed before I got there. They had no further use for the boat. With what kind of money they're making they can afford a dozen yachts like yours."

Keepnews scowled, probably displeased that people were making more money than he by illegal means.

"What's happening, if my hunch is right, is that a whole new operation is being opened up, that this is only the beginning."

"And to what do you account this?"

"Father Nick."

"Ah, Cimentini. Your nemesis."

"You might say that. But the fact is he hasn't been out of the slammer for long, he's just starting to get back in business. This is his way of overwhelming the competition right off the bat."

"So there will be more instances of piracy?"

"I wouldn't be surprised."

Keepnews appeared to consider this prospect for a brief interval. "Where's the heroin coming from, Harry?"

"Mexico."

"All of it?"

"Mexico or Colombia. But to get from one you got to go through the other. Or past it or over it."

"Yes, I see your point. Tell me, what's happening down at the department, I mean with your hearing?"

"Hasn't been scheduled yet. No one's particularly anxious to deal with it now, not Avery, not Bressler, not the D.A. They'd just as soon let it hang for a while."

"How would you like to go down to Mexico for me?"

"Depends on what you have in mind."

"Frankly, I'd like to lure these people into striking again. But this time my men will be prepared."

"Bait in other words."

"That's it." Keepnews smiled as though Harry had just made a very happy discovery. "Bait."

"May I ask you a question?"

"Fire away." This was an unfortunate choice of words, but Harry let it pass.

"Are you thinking of doing this to home in on the Mexican connection or just for revenge?"

Keepnews was not at all offended by the question. "Revenge, what do you think? I'll leave the stopping of drug traffic to the law enforcement agencies, though I can't believe they'll do a goddamn thing about it, just between you and me. All I'm after is showing whoever these people are, Father Nick or Father Time, that you can't kick Harold Keepnews in the ass and expect to get away with it. I want to do them some real harm. Not some shit operation, I'm not interested in going down to some fucking cantina in Mexico, finding four or five of their flunkies, and blowing them away. I'm sure they got a thousand guys, what do you think they get, five, ten bucks a day? You can get a million assholes that way. Lose a couple, it doesn't hurt your business at all. I'm talking about some way of getting to their vital parts. Destroying a shipment or two, now that will hurt them."

"What do you need me for? Plenty of men walking around who could do the sort of thing you want."

"You're the best. You don't go off half-cocked. I'm not

69

looking for a hit man, I don't want anything to do with them. Besides, by the time you're through you will not only be handsomely compensated, but you might very well have the satisfaction of pulling the rug out from under Father Nick."

This part of the deal did in fact attract Harry.

Sensing this, Keepnews leaned forward, "Look, you and I know, no matter how this suspension business works out, even if they reinstate you, they're never going to allow you the opportunity to get at him. Too much controversy'd be generated after that commotion at that disco downtown. Somebody gets to Father Nick, it's not going to be you. It'll be one of those assholes like what-the-hell's-his-name—Haines."

Harry avoided responding to this directly. Instead he asked Keepnews just how he meant to go about this project. He assumed that he had it all figured.

And he did. "Basically, I'm going to buy myself another boat, a cutter maybe, nothing too elaborate."

"Don't want to lose out too much if it's hijacked or goes down?"

"You got it. Then I'll spread the word we're looking for a crew, hire the best that comes around, then set sail down into Mexican waters. It's that simple."

"Nothing's that simple. What do you do, tell the men they're being set up for dope runners when you're hiring them or do you wait until they're out in the middle of the Pacific?"

"I don't think we tell them at all. Won't help them to know."

"Might save their lives."

Keepnews shrugged. This might not have been high on his list of priorities. "If they're warned in advance we lose before we're half a knot from land. I'll make sure of arms on board, and I have a man in mind I'd want to skipper the vessel. I'd let him in on it. He's a friend, completely trustworthy. So he'd know. And naturally you'd know."

"If I come along."

"I sure hope you do, Harry."

"All right, suppose your plan works, what's it going to accomplish if all that happens is you waste the jokers who try to steal your ship? You said before that's not what you're aiming for. How are you going to get close to the heroin?"

This problem did not seem to disturb Keepnews in the least. "Eventually we'll work these things out, Harry. I am not unaware of the obstacles facing me. But as you know I am a determined man. I seldom lose at what I attempt. So you let me do the worrying about these matters. All you have to do is say yes."

"I want to think on it."

"Yes, I expect you'd want to. That is sure fine with me. About how long you figure this thinking is going to take?"

"Tomorrow morning, that be soon enough for you?"

Keepnews' face registered some astonishment.

"You could take a couple of days if you'd like."

"No sense procrastinating, is there?"

Keepnews was about to show him out. Harry told him not to trouble himself, he looked like he was enjoying the comfort of his wicker chair too much.

"Suit yourself," Keepnews said. "Talk to you in the morning."

Harry was halfway through the house and out the door when he heard someone address him.

"You have a pleasant chat?"

Harry started, looked around, trying to ascertain where the voice was coming from.

Then Wendy appeared, wearing a light lavender caftan, her face partially obscured by the shadows of the stairway.

"Hello, Wendy, how are you?"

"Bored."

"A universal condition," Harry remarked, about to turn away and continue for the door. Wendy had the effect of unnerving him, not simply because she was so attractive but more because she seemed to want something from the world, from him in particular. But instead of making her interests clear, she chose to be coy about them. Harry did not like guessing games.

"Are you running away from me?"

"I was in the process of leaving your husband, not running away from you."

She was now moving down the stairs, bare feet silent against stone steps. "Ex-husband."

"Not yet," Harry reminded her.

"A mere technicality."

She approached him. Light was pouring in through high-arched windows in back of her, igniting her caftan so that it reduced the thin summer material to transparency. There was nothing Harry could discern that she wore underneath.

"Well, so long as we're not getting on each other's nerves, I suppose that's what's important."

"Oh, but we are. Didn't you hear what Harold said? He's a man determined never to lose."

"You overheard our conversation?"

"Every word." Her smile was a dangerous thing. So was the caftan. Harry was relieved when she stepped away from the light. Relieved and disappointed. She sat down on a couch—there were three to choose from in the enormous room—and asked Harry if she could get him something.

"Your husband—ex-husband, excuse me—already provided me with a drink."

After his flight from his hospital bed he'd neglected to eat anything. The alcohol in his system, having nothing to sponge it up, had gone straight to his head, which had suffered enough lately.

"I see. That's how we are around here, we vie for the position of host. Needless to say, Harold generally wins."

"But not always."

"There are some things Harold, even with all his money, will never have. Nature is occasionally more bountiful than real estate deals."

Harry gave her a searching look. "I noticed," he said.

"Are you familiar with a place called Lord Jim's?"

"On Polk? I've passed by it, why?"

"Do you think you could meet me there at five-thirty this evening?"

"I don't think so."

"Other plans?" She did not sound surprised by Harry's refusal.

"Something like that." Other plans included sleep because right now he could barely keep his eyes open.

He started toward the door. Wendy didn't move from the couch. She called after him, "Harry, did you like the flowers?"

He stopped. "So you're the one?"

"I'm the one."

"Very pretty flowers. Thank you."

He took another few steps before she brought him to a stop again. "Did the police tell you who called them and told them the *Hyacinth* was going down?"

"Why do you ask?"

"Well, did they?"

"They didn't know." Harry was looking at her real carefully. "Anonymous caller," he added.

"Not so anonymous now." She did not let Harry get a word in. "And did they tell you who pulled you out of the bay?"

So, Harry thought, my mysterious admirer turns into my mysterious rescuer too. This was getting very complicated. "What time did you say? Five-thirty?"

She nodded, and at last he was free to leave.

Chapter Eight

Lord Jim's, on the corner of Polk and Broadway, was not the sort of place Harry was used to frequenting or felt particularly comfortable in. It was a place where ferns

73

and plants with long-winded Latin names climbed and hung and drooped from every niche and crevice, their growth probably inhibited by the rock music pulsing out from some of those same niches and crevices. Tiffany lamps and what rays of the sun got through the stained-glass windows provided most of the light in the room. There was only space at the bar. The settees and the couches were filled with couples who radiated such good health that Harry had half a mind to rush back to his sickbed. Even Lord Jim himself wouldn't know what to do in this kind of atmosphere.

Wendy sauntered in. She wasn't a woman who walked anywhere. Her legs were too long for just plain walking. She had exchanged the provocative caftan for a blue blouse and white skirt that was slit way up the thigh and provided more than just a view. It was something like a spectacle.

She perched gracefully on the stool next to Harry's, addressed the bartender whom she knew by name, and ordered a gin and tonic. "You look lousy, you know that," she said to Harry. "Nothing personal."

"I don't take anything too personal, Mrs. Keepnews."

She caught the trace of sarcasm in the unexpected formality, but didn't remark upon it.

Her attention was directed elsewhere in any case. Her eyes were concentrating on the crowd that was collecting near the bar. Finally she saw who it was she was looking for. She waved. "Over here, Max! Over here!"

The man she called to was a straight-shouldered, handsome man barely past twenty. He had sandy hair and eyes of coral blue and the sullen disposition of a dog left out in the rain for too long. All he wore was a clean white T-shirt and ragged fading jeans that clung to him like it would take a knife to get them off.

"Max, meet Harry. Harry, Max."

Harry nodded in acknowledgment, growing progressively impatient the longer he sat here. He may have owed Wendy his life, but being forced to sit here among

74

these mingling veterans of the singles scene and listen to taped rock music and meet Max was a painful way of paying off his debt.

Max didn't seem too pleased to be introduced to Harry. He lowered his eyes and inspected the floor for a while. Then Wendy whispered something to him, and he withdrew into the crowd from which he'd just emerged.

"What did you want me to meet him for?"

"Simple. I'd like you to save his life."

"He looks like he's doing well enough on his own. Who do you think I am, Jesus Christ?"

She laughed, finding this very funny. "Christ saves souls. Or he's supposed to. I'm talking about his flesh and blood. He's in danger of being killed."

"That's his perogative."

"You don't understand, Harry." She took hold of his hand and held onto it for a moment longer than necessary. "It's Harold who wants to kill him."

"Oh shit."

"That's what I said. You see, Max was my lover."

"Was?"

"Was. Definitely past tense. Harold thinks that if Max's out of the way I won't have any reason for divorce. That's how he thinks."

"Revenge."

"That's right. Just like the *Hyacinth*. No one takes his boats or his woman and gets away with it. A positively medieval attitude but there it is." She looked around again, not for Max, for somebody else. "I wouldn't be surprised if he's sent somebody here to watch me. But when it comes time for the killing Harold will want to do it."

"How long were you—uh, involved with Max?"

"A few months, not long. He doesn't look like someone who'd wear long, does he?"

"No, he doesn't."

"There were a few others, I have to confess. But it was Max Harold found out about."

"Tell me, why don't you move out? Wouldn't it make life a bit easier for both of you?"

"Emotionally maybe it would. I've thought of it. But legally it gets sticky. You see, I want the house. So does Harold. If I leave I might surrender my title to it. The situation is fine with Harold because that means I'm still around. We don't share the same bed or even the same part of the house, but to the outside world we're living together and that counts a lot with Harold."

"You rich people have a shitload of problems, don't you?"

"You put it so nicely." The dangerous smile came back to her lips.

"Now you mind telling me how I'm supposed to save your precious Max's life?"

"Take him with you."

"And where am I going?"

"Mexico." She had everything figured out just like her husband. No wonder they couldn't get along, Harry thought, they were too much alike.

"Mexico?"

"You're going, aren't you? Max can come with you. We'll give him another name. He'll come on as one of the crew. He won't be any problem. He's an experienced sailor. He used to sail on the *Hyacinth* every time Harold went on one of his fishing expeditions. He knows the waters there like the back of his hand. How do you think I met him in the first place?"

"Won't Harold find out?"

"No, he's not interested in details. You and Slater— that's Slater Bodkin, the skipper Harold always hires— he'll leave you two to do the picking and choosing. I'm on good terms with Slater so there'll be no problem there either."

"Let me get this straight. You want me to take your lover—"

"Ex-lover."

"Anyone you know who isn't ex?"

76

"Sure. You."

"Great." Harry went back to looking at his drink. It was easier on the blood pressure than maintaining eye contact with Wendy. "Between you and me, aren't there simpler ways of getting Max out of harm's way? There are other boats owned by other millionaires he could ship out on."

"It wouldn't be the same."

"Of course not, this way you could do a number on your husband."

"It's more than that. What happens if Max ships out on another boat? He'll come back and still be faced with the same situation. My husband doesn't forgive or forget, honey. But if he proves himself, goes down to Mexico, and shows that he's equal to the task . . ."

"You mean if he wastes a couple of pushers instead of the other way around?"

"Well, I guess you could put it that way."

"You people are really fucking nuts, you don't mind my saying."

"Oh, I agree with you there. But you got to understand Harold. What eats at him is that I should find somebody like Max attractive. It's an insult. But if Max turns out to be well, courageous, if he has some balls, he might not be so resentful."

"I love your kind of logic, Wendy."

"So you'll do it for me?"

There was no doubt in her voice. She was convinced Harry would agree.

"Hey, I haven't even agreed to your husband's proposal, let alone yours."

"You owe me one. Considering it was your life I saved I think maybe you owe me more than one. Don't get me wrong, I'd do it again. I don't like calling in debts like this. But . . ."

"But? But what?"

"You know how it is."

"Save my ass so you can save Max's."

77

"Don't be mad. I did it because of you, not Max."

"Shit, lady, I don't think I want to understand you. Let's get out of this joint."

"Absolutely."

For all his irritation, Harry couldn't help observing what an impression Wendy was making. As soon as she got up from her stool she drew the attention of half the men in the place. She would have gotten the other half too if they could have seen beyond the ferns and the plants and the people.

As soon as they got out on Polk Street they heard a confusion of loud voices halfway up the block. From the sound of them, Harry was reasonably certain a fight was brewing. Well, it was to be expected with the heat, and he for one had no intention of investigating further to see what the trouble was.

But Wendy tensed suddenly, clutching Harry's arm. "It's Max."

"What's Max?"

"There with those men up ahead. That's his voice."

"So that's his voice, what of it?"

"Look, they're attacking him."

Harry looked and just as Wendy said, they were attacking all right, four men advancing in on him, no telling why.

Though Harry was tempted to let Max's assailants finish him off and spare Harold the obligation of killing him and himself the obligation of saving him, he knew Wendy was counting on his help.

"I'll go see what the matter is," he said, thinking that a man in his shabby condition should not get himself involved.

"Fags! All a bunch of fucking queers!" Max was shouting, apparently undaunted even though he confronted four blades which nicely caught the westering sun.

Whatever the sexual proclivities of the quartet facing down Max, they weren't taking too kindly to his abuse. Harry had no doubt that it was Max who'd provoked this altercation, thinking he could bust some ass and triumphantly walk away. Just because these four young men might have gone in for ostentatious dress, bright glossy shirts, tight pants, and bracelets, and just because they didn't look especially strong didn't mean they couldn't take Max on and make mincemeat of him.

Max kicked out at one, smacking him in his arm so hard that the man was forced to release the knife grasped in his hand. This was enough to trigger the others. They rushed him all at once. One lunged forward with his blade, scraping a bit of T-shirt and flesh off of Max, causing blood to appear, a red cloud against the background of white fabric. Max evidently didn't register the pain. He was too busy trying to knock another attacker on his ass. A third man seemed anxious to plunge his knife straight into one of Max's kidneys.

Harry was watching this without making a move. To be truthful about it, he wouldn't have minded seeing the knife hit home, but he felt a responsibility to Wendy and intervened, taking the man by surprise. He and one of his buddies turned all their attention on Harry, assuming he was an ally of Max's. Harry swept his arm forward in a swift, harsh motion. He caught a man in the neck and sent him sprawling.

By sidestepping, he avoided the other assailant completely. When the man came at him again Harry had produced his present. He didn't expect to have to use it. Usually the prospect of a .44 cartridge in one's body was sufficient to immobilize even the bravest soul.

"Aw fuck," one man said, recognizing how dramatically the odds had changed.

Max didn't seem to notice the introduction of a Magnum into the fray and was busy expending his rage by stomping one of his antagonists into the sidewalk. The man looked bruised and battered, but certainly he appeared in no worse shape than Max himself. Blood was oozing copiously out of tears in his flesh and down his arms and chest. Where there wasn't any blood there were patches of dirt and sweat. But he was so gone on adrenal-in and his own particular brand of craziness that he didn't seem to notice.

"Max, that'll be all for today," Harry said. "School's over."

Max didn't seem to hear or else he decided he'd prefer to ignore Harry's remark.

"Max!"

Max wasn't paying any attention, so Harry strode over to him and put his gun to his head. This caused Max to listen more closely. Reluctantly, he did not complete the kick he had begun. His victim rolled gratefully away, clutching his damaged rib cage with his hands.

Harry turned back to the others. A small crowd had collected to watch this unexpected drama.

"Get the hell out of here!" he urged Max's three standing antagonists.

Grabbing their prostrate friend, they did exactly that.

Max offered Harry a petulent look. He didn't like being rescued.

"I could've handled them," he muttered.

"Sure you could've, Max, sure you could've."

"You don't believe me?"

Anxious to be rid of him, Harry saw no point in arguing. "Oh, I believe you all right. Now why don't you go do something about those stab wounds. We don't want you bleeding to death."

Max regarded the blood oozing down his shirt and pants legs with indifference; he was determined to show Harry how macho he was. Nothing can touch me was his attitude. Thinking like that, Harry concluded, would get him dead one day.

Wendy approached Max now. She did not, as Harry would have suspected, blanch at the sight of his partially perforated body.

"You're going to have to get a cab because we're not about to take you to the hospital, Max."

Max glowered at her. He'd expected better. Maybe he'd had a vision of walking off into the sunset with

80

Wendy, leaving a spoor of blood behind him. Could be he'd provoked this fight just to attract her attention. Whatever his motive it wasn't working.

He grunted and walked away from them. Harry wondered when he was going to start registering the pain.

"He'll be all right," Wendy said as though this was the sort of assurance Harry was seeking. "He's always doing shit like this."

"It seems I'm already getting into practice saving his life. The way it looks to me it could become a full-time occupation."

"I do appreciate this, Harry."

He stopped her. "Wendy, I haven't said yes yet. You're not paying attention."

She shrugged, no longer interested in discussing the subject. "You hungry?"

Harry wasn't. In fact, he'd just about run clear out of energy. Intervening on Max's behalf had done him in. He felt shaky, his legs might just as well have turned into jelly for all the support they gave him.

"You're looking very pale," Wendy remarked. "Maybe you should've stayed in the hospital."

"I'm not going back there. The food they serve you is shit. Doesn't just taste bad, it's positively unhealthy. Griddlecakes and bacon for breakfast? Make you sick all over again. Though I suppose it's good for repeat business. No, all I need is just a good night's sleep."

"Where do you live?"

"I brought my car, no problem."

"You're in no condition to drive. I'll take you home." She held up her hand, unwilling to listen to any protests. "My car's right here." She gestured to the cocoa-colored BMW, which sparkled brilliantly in the dying sunlight.

Since she seemed so determined, and since he felt so drained, he did not offer any further resistence. He got in the BMW, settled back against the welcoming upholstery, and promptly fell asleep.

Day or night? No telling, not with the shades down and the curtains drawn. And hardly a noise from the street to indicate the hour: a car passing, a dog's plaintive bark, that was it. Any other sounds were blotted out by the monotonous whirring of the fan that was planted in one of the far windows.

Though Harry had no recollection of getting out of Wendy's BMW and mounting the stairs to his apartment and crawling into bed, it was obvious that he had done all these things. Because he was in bed, caught between oblivion and half-wakefulness. A weird pain was moving up his leg and settling into his thigh. The more awake he became the more of it there'd be.

Gradually, through the haze, he became aware that he was not alone in the room, and as soon as that thought impressed itself upon him, he reacted instinctively and groped for his gun. It was where he usually placed it—no matter how enfeebled he got he always knew enough to keep a weapon within reach of his bed.

His action only produced a fit of giggles. Standing at the door to the bathroom was Wendy, a disarming smile on her face and nothing on her body. In the partial darkness she was more shadow than flesh, a triumph of the human body. "Are you going to shoot me?"

Harry didn't answer. Feeling foolish, he put the gun down.

Approaching the bed, she moved quietly, almost stealthily, as though she expected her husband or one of her husband's spies to ambush her. Suddenly recalling Harold's vendetta against Max, and all those who would steal Wendy away from him, Harry wondered if he hadn't been right to grab hold of the gun before determining who there was available to use it on.

It was, however, enormously difficult keeping Harold or his vendetta in mind as he looked at Wendy. Truth was he didn't just look at her, he studied her. Her skin, he saw now that she was closer to him, was dusky, tanned everywhere from her long afternoons of sunbathing. A trickle of perspiration was visible between her breasts which swayed slightly in response to the motion of her long legs as she drew them onto the bed. Drops of moisture, like tiny jewels, glimmered on the dark triangle of hair between her legs.

"Hello, Harry," she whispered, nestling down under the covers.

"I don't think this is such a terrific idea," was what he started to say, again thinking of Harold, but it wasn't a sentence he was able to complete.

She pressed herself against him and in doing so inadvertently prodded some tender patches of flesh. But the pain was nothing compared to the pleasure she brought him. It was better than being fished out of the deep.

When he awoke again the sun was high enough in the sky to make its presence known inside Harry's apartment. Shafts of hot July light streamed in through the drawn shades and the pulled curtains.

Opening his eyes, Harry blinked. Something needed doing today, he was sure, but couldn't quite remember what it was. The other side of his bed was bare. He thought that maybe Wendy had slipped away during the night. Before he could ascertain this for certain the phone began ringing.

"Callahan," he answered in a groggy voice.

"Did I awake you, Harry?"

It was Harold. Christ, it was Harold.

"It's all right. What time is it?"

"Eight-thirty. I've been up for two hours now."

Harry had every reason to believe Harold was going to ask him what had happened to Wendy. Wendy had gone shopping and left the door open for herself or else had found the key and used it to get herself back in because she was right now stepping into the apartment, a big brown bag hugged to her chest, calling, "Harry? Are you up?" in a voice loud enough (Harry was sure) for it to be heard on the other end of the wire.

"I got us breakfast," she said before she realized he was on the phone, his hand over the mouthpiece to prevent Harold from hearing anything more incriminating. "Sorry." She clearly had no idea whom he was talking to.

"Harry, are you still there?" Either Harold had not heard his wife or else he chose to ignore her.

"I'm still here."

"I know you said you'd call me but frankly, I'm an impatient man, and I'm anxious to learn of what you decided."

"What I decided," Harry repeated dully, then remembered: the boat, the trip down to Mexico, Max. "Shit." The imprecation came automatically.

"What did you say?"

"Nothing."

"Well, I have to know. Are you with me, Harry?"

Harry looked over toward Wendy who was obliviously unpacking the goods she'd purchased, putting some of them into the depleted refrigerator and leaving others on the table. Even though she was wearing the clothes she'd had on the night before she still looked incredible, especially early in the morning. Whenever she leaned forward the slit in her white skirt would part to reveal a mesmerizing stretch of trim golden leg; he was getting fixated almost to the point of forgetting about Harold.

"Harry? Is something wrong with your connection?"

"No. Everything's fine with this connection. What the hell, sure."

"What the hell sure what?"

"What the hell, sure, I'll go to Mexico for you."

"That's great, Harry, that's marvelous. Come by later this afternoon."

Wendy, for the first time realizing who it was, turned to face Harry, then threw her hand over her mouth to keep the laughter from getting out.

Chapter Nine

"Slater Bodkin, what kind of a name is Slater Bodkin?"

Harry turned to the lean, practically emaciated figure who sat beside him on the pier, waiting to see how the man would react.

"I don't rightly know. Doesn't sound Italian, does it? It's the name my mama gave me. Not my papa. We come from what you'd call a very indeterminate heritage."

With his cap tugged down to shadow his gnarled brow and with his unlit pipe dangling between his lips, he looked the picture of the classic sea captain. He could have shipped out with the *Pequod* and gone looking for Moby Dick.

Slater loved to talk. From Harry's first introduction to the man, he'd picked up on his loquacious tendencies. "I been sailing Harold's boats for going on forty years now. I remember the first boat he had, a ketch you could barely shit in. That was before he was making any money t'all. Me and him, we'd go out fishing together. Salt water must be in our blood, I always told him. Shame about what happened to the *Hyacinth*. I'd have been on it but for the business with my back."

Here he twisted around so that Harry could better see his back. There was nothing to interest him there.

"Shot to hell. Tuna that did it. You ever try and catch a tuna, a really big tuna?"

Harry owned that he'd never done so.

"Tuna can be a bitch. Trouble is it thinks it's better than you are." Slater hesitated, spat out some phlegm that he'd kept rolling around in his mouth like chewing gum. "Generally it is. Well, one time I was foolish enough to think I could outfox one. Can't outfox no tuna, you can outlast it sometimes, but you can't outfox one, don't care what anyone says. Pulled my back something awful. Never quite recovered. Then I go ahead and do some damn thing and strain it all over again and I have to lay up for a month. Can't even walk to the can it gets so bad. Have to use one of those bedpans. It's generally humiliating."

Harry nodded. Almost nodded out. How he wondered was he going to take a stretch of days, maybe weeks, in this man's company? But he was fortunate in one thing. Slater didn't seem to need him in order to conduct a conversation; a couple of grunts, an affirmative mumble were quite sufficient for him.

"So I wasn't with the crew down Mexico way when those pirates came aboard. I've seen pirates in my time. Once off the coast of Colombia I remember I was on a ship, a couple of them bastards crept up on deck, knifed one of the watches something terrible, conked the other one over the head. You want to know what they were looking for?"

"What's that? Oh no, have no idea."

"They were looking for Colombian cash. Seems we print the damn stuff here in the States, ship it down there. Funny, how it works. All the worthless currency in the world, including our own, and we got to be printing it. Generally adds insult to injury, wouldn't you say?"

Harry said that sounded right to him.

"You done much sailing in your time?"

"Couple of motorboats now and again."

"Mmmm. Thought so. You looked to me like you got land in your blood. I can sense when somebody's done his tour and when he hasn't. So Harold wants you on as security."

"He tell you that?"

"No, old Harold he don't tell me shit. But there'd be no other reason for you, the way I see it. He's thinking there'll be more pirates, I suppose. Don't go getting the wrong impression. You fight off pirates, and that's what you're good at, well, fine with me. I'm too old, and my back's too far gone, to do that sort of shit any longer. But that don't give you the right to shirk your responsibilities running the ship when nothing exciting's happening."

"I have no intention of that."

Slater grabbed Harry's hand and shook it vigorously. "Then we'll get along just fine."

Harry now directed his eyes toward the clipboard he held in his hands. On it was a paper with the names of prospective crew members. One of them was already confirmed—Max Wilmier. It was written in Slater's handwriting.

"You been out with this joker before?"

Slater's eyebrows rose just slightly. "I take it you met Max. People when they meet Max generally don't take so well to him. Yes, I been out with him. Got nothing much for a mind, I admit you that, but he's a damn hard worker, believe it or not. Doesn't have to have anything in his belly, he'll toil in the tropical sun for you all day and all night too if you want. Never complains, never tires down. Problem is if he gets a little too much to drink, can't control him then. Always have to pull him out of altercations. T'weren't for my niece I wouldn't have signed him on."

"Wendy's your niece? You got one hell of a family, I'll tell you."

"Some girl," he said with a mysterious smile. And that, to Harry's surprise, was all he had to say on the subject of Wendy Keepnews. He might have talked a bluestreak on everything else but about Wendy he was uncharacteristically quiet.

Slater and Harry had rented an unused bait shack at the edge of the pier, just a five-minute jog down from the tourist bazaar on Fisherman's Wharf, and here they interviewed the men who came seeking work on a boat Harold hadn't gotten around to purchasing yet. Didn't matter, Harold had told them, they had only to find three men who seemed both able and minimally trustworthy.

The men came because they'd heard about the job in the local saloons or because they'd gotten wind of it down on the docks where the fish were offloaded early every morning.

Slater didn't exactly interview any of them. He was convinced that he had the intuitive powers to judge a man from the mere sight of him. Harry, who was not averse to intuition, still had his doubts regarding Slater's methods.' Especially when he'd selected his choice of a crew from among the parade of mostly scurvy-looking individuals who turned up at the pier.

One was a fellow named Booth, a husky, somewhat Neanderthal figure whose arms were festooned with tattoos testifying to a strange love for a girl named Maria and an interest in Nazi emblems. "Heavy customer all right," Slater admitted, "but he'll work his ass off and keep his mouth shut, that kind always does, and that's the way I like them."

That wasn't the way Harry liked them necessarily, not when they looked like Booth, but then he wasn't the one in charge of this part of the operation.

The second said his name was Vincent. In contrast to Booth, he was lean and nimble, with an angular face whose skin had been worked over by the sun of the tropics until it had become leathery and almost Negro-black. Vincent conceded that he had done time but that "was years ago and didn't mean shit."

"Another good worker?" Harry asked, thinking of the crew he had to cope with—Max, Vincent, Booth, and the garrulous Slater Bodkin.

"You bet," Slater said with customary authoritativeness, complacently stuffing more of his foul-smelling tobacco into his pipe.

Although there was no boat available, Keepnews had assured them that by the time they were scheduled to sail—the 20th of August—their craft would be waiting for them. And who could doubt Harold Keepnews? He made his reputation keeping his word.

But even when they got the boat there was the problem of where exactly to take it. It was one thing to direct someone into the waters off the western coast of Mexico, but presumably the object was to disembark in whatever infested town all the heroin was originating from.

This was exactly what Keepnews wished to speak to Harry about when he put through a phone call to him. A phone was the one luxury Harry and Slater could count on in their little hovel by the pier.

Slater spoke for a few minutes with Keepnews, then handed the phone to Harry, adding, "I told him we got our men."

"He want to see them?" Harry hoped that Keepnews would. One look at the whole lot of them and he'd throw them out on their collective ass—Max, Booth, and Vincent were men he wouldn't trust with a rowboat.

"Nah, he trusts my judgment."

"Of course." He put the receiver to his ear, half-expecting Keepnews to announce he'd found out about him and Wendy. But no, he sounded as smooth, as untroubled as he always did. "Harry, how're you doing? Glad to hear you've made progress down there today. Tell me, you know a place named Winnicker's? It's down somewhere near the Embarcadero, don't know where exactly, you'll have to look it up. A real dive from what I'm told."

"Not the sort of place I generally hang out."

"Didn't expect so. Anyhow, I think you ought to check this Winnicker's out. My sources say that there are men there who are substantially involved with the drug business. The mules—the couriers, you know—they frequent it, not the big-time folks. I would think that you'd have a better chance of eliciting information from them as to where the heroin is coming from in Mexico. We need a name, Harry, we need a name."

"I'll see what I can find out."

"Good man. If I couldn't depend on you who could I depend on?"

Harry hung up, not knowing exactly how to take this last remark.

Winnicker's was not easily found. It was on a street that was short, poorly lit, and in a neighborhood that looked as though it hoped everyone would simply ignore it and leave it in peace.

Harry didn't leave it in peace. There wasn't much he came in contact with that he left in what you could call peace.

Winnicker's wasn't a dive exactly, although that might have been its intention. It didn't reek of urine, for instance, which Harry took as one auspicious sign. Maybe the only one.

He didn't fit in, that was obvious from a single glance. On the other hand, this didn't much surprise him. Fitting in wasn't what he had in mind.

The customers, of whom there were a considerable number at seven in the evening, did not especially look like drug runners if drug runners can be said to have a "look." But they did exude a certain air, not of mystery but of calculation. Their eyes moved with practiced speed, took in everything, took in Harry most of all because clearly he was not a regular and had the appearance of someone who would only make trouble for them. They didn't move down the bar away from him, but they ignored him deliberately, muting their voices in his vicinity.

Then, suddenly, one man, who was probably wired on speed or going through a nervous breakdown, rushed up to Harry and said, "Hey, I know you!" From his voice you couldn't tell whether this was a good thing or a bad thing.

He was thin as they come, emaciated was more like it, all angles and bones with eyes that were beginning to burn holes in their sockets.

Harry was not prepared for recognition. He scrutinized the joker in front of him, thinking that there was in fact something familiar about him.

"Chuck," said the man now, "Chuck Loomis." He stuck out his hand. "Don't you remember me?" Disappointment tinged his voice.

"I'm not sure I do . . ."

90

"You fuckin' arrested me in 1975. Assault with a dangerous weapon."

"Ah hah." This to Harry did not seem like reasonable grounds for a great friendship. The more he studied Chuck Loomis, the more his memory cooperated in conjuring up the incident in question.

"You do remember, don't you?"

"Yes, I certainly do." Especially since the assault with a dangerous weapon had been directed against himself. Left a large gash in his left cheek, hurt like hell for a week.

"Sent away for five years."

Now it's coming, Harry thought, prepared for an outburst of anger, a demand for restitution, a vicious threat.

"Served all your time?" A harmless question he figured.

"Three years of it. Good behavior. But it wasn't so bad. I mean I don't hold it the fuck against you, you know what I'm saying? Some people, they'd get right on your fucking case, but I'm not some people. I was doing shit on the street, I get inside, well, I got a roof over my head, friends in the yard, I was head of the tennis team there. Wouldn't believe it from looking at me, but I was one hell of a tennis player. Watched TV, smoked a couple of Js before I went to sleep nights. Not a bad life considering the circumstances, you know what I'm saying? And I learned a lot of shit, got myself all lined up once I was on the street again."

Harry could imagine just what sort of education the man had acquired in prison and to what use he'd put it now that he was free.

"Now it's not that I was grateful for you busting me. It's a little bit hard working up a spirit of gratitude for somebody who's sent you away for a fin, you know what I'm saying?"

Harry had a very good idea.

"But for a cop I figured you weren't so bad. I liked your manner, believe it or not. I says to myself, 'Chuck, this is one straight dude. He bears watching!' Now I'm a well-educated man, been through three years of college, though you wouldn't know from looking at me. Majored in political science, you want to try that on for size? So I keep up, I read the newspapers. I see your name, I remember it, I read on. So what do I find out? You're in a shitload of trouble. They fucking suspended you over some shit. That Father Nick character, eh?" His voice abruptly fell lower. "There are dudes in here, they owe Father Nick, but there are dudes here, like me, we hate his fucking guts. You know what I'm saying? We got our territory parceled out, we got our business just like you got yours—or had yours—and this Father Nick, he walks out of the slammer, shoves his butt in, announces that he's doing the kingpin number. Well, fuck him, I say."

As he continued, Harry deduced three things—one that Loomis was probably on speed and couldn't shut up, two that he'd perceived in Harry a possible ally because he too was in trouble with the law, and three that anyone who busted Father Nick couldn't be all bad.

"They let Father Nick walk." Harry decided to stick with neutral statements—seemed safer that way.

"Father Nick will always walk. Like that fellow, what's-his-damn-name in New York, spade pusher, carried $75,000 for spare change, he got out on bail, maybe half a mil, maybe a mil, and he just went and disappeared. The Father Nicks of the world always walk unless somebody stops them cold, guts their insides, and stuffs 'em."

"Any idea who's going to do that?"

Chuck Loomis allowed his inflamed eyes to survey the inhabitants of Winnicker's. "No one hereabouts I'll tell you. Mules got a philosophy. They don't interfere. There's a job they do it. The time will come they'll all be working for Father Nick. You should know there's no such thing as loyalty in this business once the cash stops flowing."

Harry acknowledged that he understood the truth of this. "Tell me something, Chuck," he continued, trying to sound very casual, "is Father Nick using the same source or is he opening up another one? I hear he's operating in Mexico these days."

Loomis hesitated, but not because he was apprehensive about divulging what information he had, it was just that he wasn't so sure about how true it was. "Now you got to know one thing, I've been out of this business for some time . . ." He did not realize that he had just contradicted his assertion of a few minutes before that he'd been set up right after emerging from prison. Probably needed to protect himself. "So I can only tell you what I hear the talk is. And the talk is Carangas."

"Carangas?"

"That's what I hear. Down on the western coast somewhere. Never been there myself. Probation officer don't like me traveling. I never get farther than Oakland. Besides, it's new, Carangas, not the town, just the use they're making of it. Like the Wild West, everyone with guns, knives. You'd probably love it."

"I don't suppose it gets written up much in the travel brochures."

Chuck Loomis liked this remark and howled with laughter. This drew some reproachful looks from the others in the house.

"Say, can I buy a drink for my arresting officer?"

Harry saw no reason to remain any longer in Winnicker's now that he had the information he had come for but, before he could refuse the offer Loomis had already turned to the bartender. "Give my friend whatever he's drink—" He didn't get any further. Harry looked at him. Loomis wasn't doing so well, his body had stiffened, and his face, pale to begin with, had gone absolutely livid: a hue well beyond where the rainbow ends. He clutched both hands on the edge of the bar, desperate to keep himself upright. It was not going to work. He tottered like a child taking its first steps, then released his feeble hold on the bar. Dazedly, he stepped aside from Harry and began lurching out into the center of the bar, knocking against a table, much to the consternation of the two leather-jacketed men drinking there. Then, without warning, he spun around, deciding on the opposite direction, thinking possibly that the door might be a better option. As he staggered, a slight, barely perceptible trickle of blood down his pants leg began to turn into a thickly swelling ooze. A jagged trail of glistening red followed him.

The problem was seeing where all this blood was coming from because of the jacket he wore. But Harry had no doubt that Loomis had been knifed. There was of course no telling who'd been responsible. Everyone at the bar looked equally innocent—and equally guilty—their eyes were all fixed on the uncertain progress Loomis was making toward the exit. It was as though he felt he could be free of his pain if he could only get some fresh air. This therapy would not be sufficient. Not that it mattered. Loomis did not have enough energy left in him to attain the door. He stopped, turned again so as to face the Winnicker's regulars expectantly waiting for his death. Then, drawing himself up, he seemed about to curse them all for their iniquity. But when he opened his mouth to speak the words he got out were submerged in a bubble of blood that smeared his lips and chin all at once. With a final shudder he crumpled to the floor. Even then he seemed not to have made his mind up about dying; he was on his knees, like a penitent at confession; his eyes were closed but you could see he was still living because tears—of pain, of anger, of regret—still leaked from them. He even managed to wipe his mouth free of some of the blood with the back of his shirtsleeve in an attempt to recapture some shred of dignity. That done, he decided all at once to give up. He died like that right on his knees.

"We can call the cops now," the proprietor, a lug of a man with a Texan hat and a bountiful beard, informed the bartender. Harry had the impression that incidents like this were not all that infrequent. As soon as he'd made his announcement—which was directed to the customers as much as to the bartender—the bar began to clear.

Harry had not moved the whole time. There'd been nothing he could have done for Loomis, and while he had his suspicions as to which one of the men here had knifed him, he could not be absolutely certain. Moreover, the murderer would have backup, and Harry was not prepared for a struggle against such formidable odds. This was enemy territory. He did much better on neutral turf.

But he did have to assume that Loomis was killed for his habit of talking too much to the wrong people. Being one of those wrong people, Harry recognized that he too was in danger. Not here though. They—whoever "they" were—would not risk perpetrating two murders in the same bar on the same evening. Especially when one of them would involve a cop—even if that cop was on suspension.

Once beyond the vicinity of Winnicker's though, it was natural to expect his unknown antagonists to strike.

No matter. He had no impulse to linger on here, hoping they'd all go away by the time he left. He was not, however, fast enough out the door to avoid the police coming in. They'd responded to the belated call far more quickly than Harry had anticipated. He had not wished to deal with his colleagues at this juncture.

Especially with Bob Togan.

Togan looked so astounded to see Harry here, of all places, that he gave him a far more searching glance than he did the corpse at his feet. He might be viewing an apparition. "Harry?" he inquired tentatively, possibly hopeful that he might be mistaken, that it might be somebody who just looked like Harry.

"How are you doing, Bob?"

It was Harry. Togan seemed gravely disappointed.

"You wouldn't want to tell me what you're doing here, would you?"

He did not sound remotely hopeful.

"No."

But on the other hand he wasn't prepared for such a brusque rebuff. "Wait a minute, you can't just walk out on me like this! What happened here?"

"You can see for yourself. Some joker took a knife to this guy on the floor. His name is Chuck Loomis, did time for assault once. Probably a drug runner. Who did it is something I couldn't rightly tell you. Now you know all I know."

Togan clearly meant to question those few customers remaining in the bar, but he would obtain nothing from them and he probably already knew that. The murderer had fled, and all anyone would ever say was that they'd seen nothing. Why make such a big deal about another barroom brawl? And that would be the end of it.

Harry stepped around Loomis because it was not possible to step over him. "Keep me out of this one, Bob," he said in parting.

"I'm always keeping you out of shit, Harry!" Togan called after him. "Why don't you do me a favor and keep yourself out now and then?"

Harry didn't reply, he was already out the door.

Chapter Ten

Though the sun continued to blaze in the west, a pale orange star in a grayish summer sky, darkness had already taken root here on this obscure street. Taller buildings guarded it from too much light. In the near distance Harry could make out the bellow of foghorns as the ferries sluggishly made their way into port.

Harry had to interpret the shadows—somewhere along this block he was certain Chuck Loomis' killer was waiting for him. His car was the only vehicle parked up ahead. It was as conspicuous as its owner.

That nothing happened to him so surprised him that he began to think he'd done something wrong. The possibility of a bomb planted in his car occurred to him, but he would just have to risk it.

No sooner had he inserted his key into the lock than a sharp ringing sound disrupted the lazy silence of the street. Harry dropped down instantly, sliding underneath his Buick—or rather the SFPD's Buick because they had neglected to take it away from him for the duration when they had relieved him of his badge. It still took him a moment longer to identify the sound. It had been a single gunshot richocheting off the roof of the car. His assailant was positioned on top of one of the buildings, overlooking the street.

But which one? From his poor vantage point he couldn't even raise his eyes high enough to see past the third stories of the tenement houses.

Harry reached up and extracted the key from the lock. The gesture did not provoke the gunman into firing again. With the key in hand, Harry inched his way under the car, keeping his chest against the pebbly bed of the street, until he reached the other side.

But just as he brought his head into view two rounds plowed into the door he'd been about to open, causing two indentations, one above the other in the steel surface. Harry sensibly withdrew under the car.

These shots, Harry surmised, came not from a rooftop but from someone on the ground, possibly concealed in a thick ailanthus bush on the opposite side of the street.

He did not move immediately. And by the same token the unseen gunmen did not fire. The squad cars might still be parked in front of Winnicker's at the other end of the block, for all Harry knew, but he could not depend on Togan for help. Actually, he'd prefer not to involve Togan at all if he could help it.

Instead, he listened carefully for the sound of any approaching car. Although it would provide him with only a very few seconds, a passing vehicle would still give him cover. Unfortunately, the street wasn't heavily trafficked, so it required several minutes before he'd managed to get his key in the door, unlock it, and withdraw the key again so as not to alert his friend tucked away in the ailanthus bush as to what he had planned.

He felt that he had some luck coming to him by now, and his reckoning proved right. For now there appeared, with rumbling motor and spewing exhaust stack, a huge mother of a truck: it was bearing a refrigeration unit that seemed half a block long. Also, it wasn't moving very fast.

Delighted with this unexpected opportunity, Harry slid out from under his shelter and threw open the door, closing it just as he pitched down in the seat, careful to keep his head out of view from either side.

When the truck had passed, and there was no fire, Harry realized that his ruse had worked. Either that or his assailants had given up and gone away entirely. Well, he would soon find out.

There was no way of keeping the ignition muffled once he'd started it. But that didn't worry him. He got the Buick into motion, his foot firmly on the gas, his hands gripping the bottom crescent of the steering wheel. All he could see was a lot of sky through the windshield and not much street. Never mind—the last thing he was concerned about was crashing into something—so long as it wasn't something with sufficient resistance to stop him for good.

The glass on his right side did not particularly enjoy welcoming high-calibered rounds, which had a tendency to turn it into the consistency of cellophane. The glass on his left side wasn't any more receptive. Well, that answers that, Harry thought, they're still out there.

The windshield was transformed within moments into an elaborate spiderweb, riddled with holes. Glass splinters bombarded Harry as he attempted to guide the Buick into safer territory. Out of the corner of his eye he observed himself in the rearview mirror. He saw a face he barely recognized: it was the face of a haggard man whose flesh kept bursting out in spots of red; it was as though he were sweating blood. He decided that he'd rather not look.

The gunman on the ground, possibly realizing that he wasn't going to hit Harry, was discharging his fire into the Buick's tires with such fierce accuracy that the car listed right as the rubber on both wheels on that side blew. Bad enough driving a car without seeing where you're going; it was worse with two tires disabled.

The Buick banged along noisily, its speed reduced dramatically. Still, Harry was able to get beyond the range of fire, though this did not mean that he was necessarily safe. He did, however, enjoy the luxury of raising his head above the dashboard. Not that this did much good since with the windshield so cracked and ruptured, it was a little like trying to see through gauze.

Which might have explained why he failed to notice the red Impala that was waiting for him at the next intersection. It shot out as soon as the Buick came into sight, blocking Harry's path long enough for the man on the passenger side to fire his 30-30 straight into the car.

But this blast, while tearing a huge portion of the battered windshield from its moorings and further criss-crossing Harry's equally battered face with cuts, did not halt Harry's progress.

To be sure, the concussive roar of the shotgun explosion and the terrific protest of glass and metal it caused was shock enough to Harry—especially because he had no way of knowing it was coming—but his instinctive reaction was to depress the gas pedal straight to the floor. The wounded Buick, with one final burst of energy, spun crazily into the intersection and caught the Impala in its rear at such a high speed that it locked into it securely and, more than that, gripped it in its motion so that the Impala was forced to turn with it.

As the driver of the Impala fought to extricate himself, he misjudged his distance or his timing or something and jumped the curb of a traffic island, sweeping a traffic light into the street. But this maneuver, however clumsy, did not succeed in freeing the Buick which dragged along behind it, swinging uncontrollably to the right and to the left.

Harry, having given up on the idea of trying to drive his car any longer, had simply crouched down, waiting for the buffeting to come to an end so he could leap out.

Police sirens could now be heard, a thickening dissonant chorus directly behind them.

This must have decided the two men in the Impala. Recognizing that they could not dispose of the albatross the Buick represented, they brought their vehicle to a halt dead center of the street and got out, presuming they had sufficient time to escape on foot.

As soon as Harry felt the Buick come at last to rest, he forced open the door and half-jumped, half-fell out of the car. Clearing his eyes of the blood that tended to mist them over, heedless of the myriad pinpricks of pain that attacked every inch of his face, he moved agilely, gripping his new Magnum in hand. Time, he thought, to break it in.

The Impala's driver saw him first. He was doing something you should never do—look back to see if someone's gaining on you. Harry was gaining on him. The driver did not expect to see Harry alive. Harry did not necessarily look alive with all the blood coating his face and threatening to stain his shirt and jacket, but he certainly moved as though he were. And no ghost had the aim he did. The driver learned this to his dismay as a round from the Magnum caught him in the side, between the ninth and tenth rib. The force took him and flung him into the air, then dropped him unceremoniously on the cement. His companion, still with the shotgun, stopped, astonished to see how things were developing.

"Sumabitch, sumabitch!" he kept yelling at Harry, outraged that he should still be alive. He turned his 30-30 on him and discharged it while still in motion with the result that he succeeded only in adding a crater-sized hole to the traffic island.

Harry, having a great deal of respect for the 30-30, had flattened himself just in case and now had to waste time in picking his body up and doing something significant with it. The man with the shotgun was sprinting in the direction of the bay. It was obvious he was too preoccupied by the business of fleeing to fire his shotgun. Actually, he no longer seemed conscious of the shotgun in his hand though it was not an object easily forgotten about.

People crossing his path stopped and gazed at him inquisitively. Most, however, were smart enough to stand aside and watch him from a respectable distance. Those who didn't see him coming found him barreling down on them, ready to knock anyone aside who got in his way.

But if a man carrying a loaded shotgun was a spectacle, Harry was no less of one, his face a mask of blood, his clothes smeared with more of the same. One look at him and you'd think his injuries were sure to be fatal.

Sirens continued to signal the impending presence of the police, but thus far no one could see them. They were still back at the traffic island scrutinizing the damage to the Buick and Impala and to the Impala's now-deceased driver.

The pursuit continued beneath an overpass. It was darker here and emptier, filled with the rumblings of the traffic piling off the Oakland Bay Bridge into the city. For several moments Harry lost sight of his quarry. Leaning in against one of the massive cement columns that served to prop up the overpass, Harry strained to see what had happened to him.

He was rewarded for his vigilance. The gunman had now broken for an exit ramp, apparently oblivious of the fact that there was no space provided on the ramp for pedestrians. What's more, he was going against the traffic.

Harry chased him, hoping that he could bring this to a halt soon because his energy was rapidly depleting.

The gunman's sudden appearance on the off-ramp was greeted by a cacaphony of horns as surprised motorists tried to avoid running him over. Which was too bad;

Harry wouldn't have minded if somebody did his work for him this time.

When the gunman looked back and saw Harry he repeated his favorite phrase: "Sumabitch! Sumabitch!" he called and drew to a stop right at the crest of the ramp. With only a foot or so between him and the oncoming traffic he loosened his 30-30 on Harry who was advancing toward him.

Harry couldn't duck, didn't have the time. Instead he had to do a quick step to the right which put him in line with the cars rushing down from the freeway. A green Chrysler with a U-Haul van trailing behind it screeched crazily as the driver sought to brake before he found Harry under his tires. The look he gave Harry was almost as murderous as the shell from the 30-30 which pulverized a portion of one of the cement pillars—but not enough to jeopardize the stability of the overpass.

"What the fuck you think you're doing?" the driver of the Chrysler shouted, somehow failing to register the percussive report of the shotgun blast.

Harry had no time to make the necessary explanations. He darted around to the other side of the Chrysler just as a member of a bike club, festooned with leather, his face hidden behind faintly ominous, but also faintly silly, goggles, came zooming down the ramp so fast that he could not stop in time and crashed headlong into the rear of the U-Haul. He was thrown forward and up and tumbled in the air like a young bird first experimenting with its wings. When he came down he cracked first his helmet, then his skull, and lay unmoving in the pool of blood that was leaking out of both his ears.

More cars were coming down the ramp, and their drivers weren't any better prepared to find their passage blocked than the motorcyclist had been.

One car after another began to go into a skid, then plow into the vehicle ahead of it. The driver from the Chrysler emerged, horror-struck to see what had happened to the cyclist. He would have abused Harry for causing all this carnage were Harry still available. But Harry was already heading up the ramp, ignoring the pile-up that was developing as bumpers collided and taillight glass smashed all to the accompanying din of blaring horns and screaming drivers who couldn't figure out how they'd gotten into this mess or how they were going to get out of it.

The gunman was now running on the freeway, keeping as close to its perimeter as he could. To give himself time, he would at intervals stop and fire his shotgun. He clearly did not expect to hit Harry—his aim was far too wide of its target—but he did force Harry to drop down.

What the gunman did not anticipate was the appearance of a passing police cruiser. But there it was, its blinking signal light slicing him with blades of red. The cruiser pulled up right beside him. The gunman didn't wait to see what the two officers inside would do. Instead, forgetting Harry for the time being, he levelled his 30-30 straight into the window on the passenger side of the cruiser and fired.

There was no telling what the cops had been thinking when they pulled over. Possibly they'd just noticed a man running on the bridge and hadn't noticed the shotgun. But it didn't matter now. The blast took the first officer directly in the face, blowing his head clean out the other window and onto the bridge. The same blast caught his partner in the neck and upper chest, its force scarcely diminished by the flesh and bone it had first to travel through. Both men were dead instantly.

All this while, Harry had gained on the man. He must have sensed this for he swung the 30-30 around and fired again, not aiming, just assuming that Harry would be somewhere within his sights. He did not realize that Harry had circled around and, veering out into the traffic, had crept up behind the other side of the police cruiser.

"Over here!" Harry said, the Magnum extended in his hands and resting against the roof of the cruiser.

The gunman looked toward him in utter bewilderment.

A little belatedly, he thought of thrusting his shotgun through the open window of the cruiser and shooting Harry. Whatever his next thought was it was his last.

The .44 hit him at the top of his skull, right in a glimmering bald spot which made for a perfect target. Blood, like oil, erupted from the surface. The gunman was driven back by the shot—and though he didn't leave the ground, it seemed that at any moment he might. Then his body, propelled backward, reached the edge of the bridge and, not being content to stop right there, continued farther and plummeted into the bay.

Harry regretted having not delivered him to the bottom of the sea earlier—before he'd gotten the two cops—but even killers had their season, and sometimes you couldn't do anything to them until that season ran out.

As additional police cruisers pulled onto the bridge, Harry turned and trudged wearily back to San Francisco. He figured he'd like to get someplace where he could stop losing blood.

Chapter Eleven

"Haven't seen you in a few days, where you been keepin' yourself?"

As Slater Bodkin probably wasn't interested in a response, Harry had no intention of giving him one. Slater looked up, noticing the Band-Aids that were strategically positioned on Harry's face. He frowned. "Accident I reckon," he said.

"That's right."

"An automobile?" Slater made every syllable of the word count.

"You got it."

"Young man like you ought to be more careful." That said, he promptly lost his fascination with Harry's condition. "Out there, you see it!" He swept his arm back to the right.

"The boat?"

"It's ours. Or to be precise, it's Harold's. But generally speaking, it's ours for the duration. Handsome, ain't she? I'd say close to two hundred thousand for her. 'Fraid our Harold got carried away again."

It had the look of a craft worth that much. It stretched out to a shade longer than forty feet and gleamed whiter than 1600 Pennsylvania Avenue, with a flush aft-deck configuration.

For a boat that might well be sacrificed, it was an expensive proposition. Keepnews could always replace the crew, including him, but the boat?—he was going to have to sell a hell of a lot of shopping malls and condominiums to keep affording yachts like this one.

"She's got two staterooms forward, a master stateroom aft," Slater was saying. "Plenty of space for everyone. Got a saloon and a nice little galley where Max'll have everything he needs."

"Max?"

"Great cook, Max is. You should see what he does with flounder. Only trouble is he likes everything hot."

"Hot? Spicy hot?"

"Sometimes he goes overboard." He chuckled deeply at his own little joke. "I mean on the food. I remember a couple of times our lips were running blood. But if you can get beyond the hot the taste is real fine."

This was going to be some sea voyage, Harry thought, lips bleeding, stomach churning. Just thinking of Max, he lost his appetite.

"Best thing about her though is the windows. Half-inch Du Pont Abscite. Bulletproof!"

"Nice thing to know."

With Slater's arch manner and unrelenting chatter it was hard to tell what the man was thinking.

"Go take a good look at her. She'll be your home the next few weeks."

Harry sauntered down the length of the pier, striding

up to the boat. He was now close enough to make out the name Keepnews had christened the boat with. It was certainly appropriate.

CONFRONTATION the dark Roman characters on the hull spelled out.

Maybe not yet, Harry considered, but soon enough.

When he got back to the other end of the dock he saw that Slater was no longer by himself. He was with his niece. Wendy. A revealing purple halter allowed an ample glimpse of clean tan flesh above and below; her cut-offs ended abruptly, extremely high on her thighs. Her hair was tied back and covered by a yellow handkerchief. Her eyes flashed at him from behind big oval glasses tinted the same shade as her halter. She waved to him.

"You like Harold's new toy?"

"An impressive piece of machinery," he admitted.

"Harold bought it yesterday, decided to bring it down here and show Slater. Sort of a test run. You know how Harold gets. Once the urge strikes, he has to do everything all at once. I don't think he ever waited in line for anything in his life."

Slater grinned and chomped down on his pipe.

Wendy strode up to Harry and, taking him by the arm, drew him away from Slater. "How come you never called? I was expecting you to." She wore a petulant expression that reminded Harry of a cross child.

"Well, I got kind of caught up in things."

This stopped her. She gently raised her hand and touched his face.

"Oh yes. I'm sorry, I'd forgotten. Are you going to be permanently scarred?" She seemed suddenly worried about how his face would look once the bandages came off.

"I don't suspect that I'll be entering any beauty contests any time soon if that's what you mean. But I probably won't look in much worse shape than I was when I started."

"My problem is that I'm too selfish, think just of myself."

Harry didn't contradict her. It was *her* problem. One of them at any rate.

She went on. "It must have been awful to have gone through that."

She might have been referring to the running battle that had continued outside of Winnicker's, but Harry wasn't absolutely certain. A woman like Wendy tended to be on the oblique side. "I can see where you wouldn't have had a chance to get in contact with me."

"So Harold told you what happened?" Harry was interested in seeing how information was communicated in the Keepnews' house.

"Oh no." She gave a bitter laugh. "Harold never tells me anything. Or else what he does say is not always the whole truth. But I have my ways of finding out what's going on."

"I'm sure you do." Harry was developing an appreciation for her skills at ferreting out facts—not to mention fishing people out of the deep.

"Which is why I happen to know you were set up."

Harry held her in his eyes, trying to divine her thoughts. Impossible.

"You mind explaining, Mrs. Keepnews?"

She wasn't looking at him. She seemed to find the polluted waters of the bay more interesting.

"Harold found out about us. You don't think we fooled him. And like I told you before, Harold's a man who can get insanely jealous. Just as he did with Max."

The idea of being linked with Max, no matter what the context was, irritated the hell out of Harry.

"Now how did he find out?"

"I don't know. Maybe one of the men he has out following me around. He has spies everywhere."

As she continued speaking Harry began to get the feeling that she was making this up as she went along. But he couldn't be absolutely certain. "So what you're saying is that Harold decided to kill me, and he did it the easiest way he knew, by sending me to Winnicker's and having some drug runners do the job for him?"

Wendy hesitated as though she had to give this some thought, see if it jibed with the scenario she'd constructed —or was it the truth as she knew it? Then she said yes, that was how she understood it was.

"But now that I'm still among the living, he's going to let me go fishing for him off Mexico?"

She shrugged. "You might want to give it up. Mexico's just another way of getting killed."

"What about Max? I thought the idea was to save his ass."

"Max," she said dully. She seemed to have forgotten all about him. Max had a habit of slipping from memory if you didn't work hard at it.

She turned to face Harry, her eyes mysterious entities behind those lavender-tinted lenses of hers. "I don't think any harm will befall Max. He'll survive." Again she touched his face, very tentatively. "It's you I worry about."

Then she leaned close to him, pressed herself to him on tiptoes, and kissed him full on the mouth. And was gone. Like that. Ran off as though a more protracted goodbye would prove too wrenching.

Harry all at once felt very old. He walked back to where Slater was sitting. Slater pretended to have seen nothing. He too appeared to be enthusiastically studying the murky greenish waters in the vicinity of the piers. The seagulls that swooped down on the rotted wood pilings were being very noisy. Slater was being very quiet.

"So," he said, sounding very offhand, "you're going to be ready to sail Friday?"

"Friday? Thought it wasn't to be till the end of next week." Friday was just two days away.

"Moved up. Harold's orders. Friday now."

"Well," said Harry, watching a couple of squawking seagulls do a little jig in the afternoon sunlight, "as far as I'm concerned the sooner the better."

Chapter Twelve

Two days out at sea and there was already trouble. Not trouble from pirates. They might be lurking just beyond the horizon for all Harry knew, but they had yet to make themselves known. No, the trouble was all due to the crew members. One of them would have been all right, even two of them would be possible. But the combination of Max, Vincent, and Booth was deadly. The only reason, it seemed to Harry, that Vincent and Booth got along was because they hated Max so much. Without Max, they'd have been tearing at each other's throats. Max, of course, didn't like anyone, and from the way he acted you got the feeling he expected the same in response.

Slater, by temperament or sheer intestinal fortitude, seemed to be able to accommodate everyone. He never raised his voice when he was angry. He merely sucked a bit harder on his pipe and gave the miscreant a withering stare. Possibly it was because he expected people to do what he wanted that he was obeyed. Maybe it was some kind of mystical force he had acquired in the years he'd spent at sea.

Harry, on the other hand, was something of a mystery to the crew. They couldn't figure out what he was doing on the boat. Max, who knew more than the others, was especially resentful of his presence and even at the outset he'd attempted to enlist Booth and Vincent against him. But because Booth and Vincent so generally despised Max, they assumed that Harry couldn't be all bad if Max didn't like him. Not that they were inspired to strike up a friendship with Harry; that would be stretching things too far. Rather, they avoided him whenever possible, and if their paths should cross, they'd make do with a grudging nod and a mumble that might have been hello.

The three crew members occupied the two forward staterooms. Harry and Slater shared the master one aft, which worked out well enough. Usually one or the other of them was on watch, allowing each all the privacy he wanted.

So it was that Harry was alone, stretched out on one of the twin beds, staring lackadaisically up through the porthole. All he could see was blue, blue sky, blue water, blue everything. That was just fine by him—he wasn't anxious to use his eyes for anything more taxing.

Just then there was a commotion above him. He turned over in hope that whatever it was would go away. Didn't go away. Instead it just got louder. Voices began to distinguish themselves. He heard Slater yelling, and that was something he never did.

With a groan Harry lifted himself from the bed and went to see what the matter was.

Out on deck he found Max and Booth squared off. Booth was naked to the waist, which permitted a panoramic view of his gallery of tattoos. Swastikas and royal black eagles rippled each time he raised or swung his arms. In his right hand he held a speargun. Max, not to be outdone, clutched a knife in his hand. The knife, Harry estimated, was capable of going straight in one side and out the other with an inch or so left over for insurance. Max never seemed to learn. He too was naked to the waist, and here and there on his tan well-developed chest you could see where other knives had gone before, leaving behind streaks of pink and white scar tissue. Undoubtedly, some of those scars had been made that day on Polk Street before Harry had intervened.

Well, now it looked as though he was going to have to intervene again because it didn't appear that Slater was likely to get things under control. Though he was eager to mediate he was still wise enough to keep his distance, contenting himself with loud words and arms raised in appeal.

Vincent meanwhile was thoroughly enjoying the spectacle. "Stick him!" he kept urging Booth, "stick him!"

Booth had the advantage. His weapon was longer, allowing him more room in which to maneuver. But you had to give Max one thing—he was not afraid. He might be a moron, but he was a brave moron.

"What's this shit about?" Harry asked Vincent.

Vincent spat out his cigarette and said, "Booth got the runs from Max's cooking. That meat loaf last night, that was what did it."

"I had the meat loaf," Harry said. "I survived."

Vincent shrugged. "Booth's got a more sensitive stomach maybe."

Looking at him, Harry doubted that Booth had a sensitive anything.

"Cook your own shit from now on!" Max was saying.

"I'll cook you, you cocksucker, I'll roast you and eat you whole."

Booth suddenly lunged forward, baring his teeth in his attempt to show Max he meant what he said.

Vincent laughed.

"You all can go to hell," was Slater's judgment. Harry had the feeling that he'd have liked to walk away and forget the whole business, but obviously there was nowhere to walk away to.

"I don't believe this, I really don't think I believe this," Harry said. He had the vision of two dead crewmen, martyrs to lousy meat loaf.

He would have to do something. He preferred to let them grind each other into the deck, but it would be far better if they did so without the benefit of sharpened instruments.

So Harry stepped between them, knowing that all this action did was to invite getting stabbed from both sides. But for the moment he enjoyed the luxury of surprise. Neither Booth nor Max had made up their minds about what Harry's intercession meant.

"Why don't you throw down your weapons?" Harry said, his voice deliberately calm. "You want to fight, fight. God might not have given you any brains but He gave you two hands."

Booth had to think about this for a minute. Harry knew if he got one he had the other. The question was would either of them accept his suggestion?

Finally, Booth dropped the speargun into Vincent's hands. "I'm willing," he declared, leaving Max with no choice. He surrendered his blade to Slater.

Booth didn't waste any time. He delivered a nicely executed roundhouse kick straight to Max's chest, knocking the wind right out of him. For unfathomable reasons Max remained erect. You could hear him sucking frantically for breath. It was clear that if he didn't do something soon the fight would be over before it had started. Booth charged in again, battering Max with a succession of blows that sent him staggering back toward the starboard side. Max was not used to someone like Booth. Booth moved in, resolved to finish the job without further ado.

Although it surprised the hell out of Harry, he realized that he wanted Max to win. He disliked Max intensely, wished he'd never laid eyes on him much less accepted the responsibility for saving him from Harold's wrath. But when the choice was Max or Booth, Harry decided to go with the lesser of two evils.

The lesser of two evils wasn't faring very well. The only reason he was still standing was because he had the gunwales to prop him up. Still the gunwales weren't very high, and it would only take Booth a few solid punches to send him crashing into the Pacific where, already bloodied, he might prove too much of a temptation to the sharks who made their home there.

Maybe he slipped, maybe he purposely stepped out of the way, it was hard to tell, but whatever impulse guided Max it was obviously the correct one. By moving to the left he managed not only to avoid a blow that might have dropped several front teeth down his throat but he also succeeded in unbalancing Booth. Booth, having expected Max to remain in one place, had lunged forward. But all he found himself hitting was thin air. And because he was in motion, he could not stop, and so propelled he slammed his belly against the gunwales, grimacing in pain.

Max, surprised to find he had an advantage, had recovered sufficient wind to drive a punch into the side of Booth's head. Instantly Booth's left ear turned deep scarlet. Booth half-turned, only to receive a left hook that found its resting place directly underneath his chin. Having not really gotten his balance back, Booth was hurled up against the wall of the pilothouse. His head made a loud cracking sound when it hit. Both his hands clutched his throat. For several moments he remained unmoving. Max's blow must have temporarily jeopardized his air supply. He was gasping as hard as Max had been just a half a minute or so before.

Max, moving very slowly as though he were already immersed in water, now stepped forward and began to rain Booth with several more blows. Booth still could not react, and the only protective gestures he made were to turn his head and twist his body to diminish the target area Max had to work with.

Vincent didn't like how this fistfight was developing. Harry could see that he was anxious to intervene on his friend's behalf. Not being constrained by the rules established for the fight, he thrust out the speargun Booth had given him. Then he started his advance toward the two struggling men.

Harry reached forward, gripping him by the arm. "I wouldn't do that, Vincent."

Vincent glared at Harry. The tip of the speargun was now turned toward him. Slater noticed this and, with Max's knife in hand, began to circle around just in case Harry required assistance.

This was one instance Harry was determined not to resort to fire-power. Producing a gun would only invite further suspicion as to what his role was on the *Confrontation,* and he refused to take that risk unless it was absolutely necessary.

Seeing that Harry had no intention of backing down,

Vincent grumbled and lowered the speargun. He then went back to being a spectator.

Booth had by this point recuperated to the point where he was giving as good as he got. Neither of the combatants was making much headway mainly because they were both running out of energy. The punches were landing with negligible force, arms and legs were moving with such sluggish speed that it looked as though their bodies would soon shut down altogether.

Then Max, finding his second wind, let loose a fury of punches that thudded clumsily against Booth. Still, they carried a certain power to them and had the effect of driving Booth back against the wall of the pilothouse again. When Booth attempted to regain a more strategically viable position in the middle of the deck, Max sent a straight punch into his stomach. All at once Booth went down, because of the impact or because he'd lost his footing on a patch of water. He lay outstretched for a few seconds, stunned and indignant that he should be down at all. Then, with difficulty, he hoisted himself aloft again.

Slater now came forward, holding up his hands to keep the two contestants separated. "That's it, that's the end of it."

"What the fuck do you mean, Slater, that's it? I slipped." Booth looked to Vincent to support his opinion. "You saw that, I just slipped. This asshole didn't fucking knock me down."

Max, not being content with Slater's judgment of victory, stood there grinning, confident he could return Booth to the surface of the deck with no trouble at all. His ugly smirk dared Booth to come at him again.

No question about it, Harry thought, Max was an asshole. Now that the fight appeared over he could go back to despising him. It made him feel better.

"You men want to keep up, well, go ahead. But I'm raising anchor and getting on with the business of sailing south."

"Forget it, Booth, we'll have our chance later," Vincent said.

Booth, his face smeared with sweat and blood that still dribbled out of his nostrils, regarded his antagonist darkly. Then he turned defiantly toward Slater and Harry, muttering, "Sure will have our chance later. Sure will." It seemed that he was threatening not just Max but Harry and Slater as well. This did not surprise Harry. He was beginning to think that they would have to abandon the two mutinous crewmen in Mexico, let them find their way back on their own, because he could not see how they could be counted on once they started home. That is, *if* they started home.

Booth and Max got themselves cleaned up and then resumed work as though nothing had happened between them.

Slater was silent for the next hour afterward. He stood at the wheel, casting his dimming eyes toward the sea, staring straight into a setting sun that carved out a blood-red trail across the horizon. At last he spoke to Harry, though he never allowed his eyes to leave the Pacific.

"Wrong chemistry. Generally you get a better chemistry among a crew than we got here."

"I'll grant you that."

"None of them alone'd be bad. Putting the three together!" He shook his head gravely. "But you never can tell, can you?"

Harry agreed that this was the case.

"Still you know that Booth he had a point."

"Oh?"

"That meat loaf last night was shit."

Chapter Thirteen

The speedboat—a Cigarette—reached the target area at quarter past the hour. The sun had been gone from this part of the globe for several hours. The darkness was nearly total—the half-moon had already sunk below the horizon.

Milano finished what was left of his coffee and went up on deck. There waiting for him was Conrad, a humorless albino who'd once played bass for a Southern rock and roll band. He was strumming on a guitar now, serenading the Pacific with a song about a lost lover. Milano was tired of songs about lost lovers. Ever since Conrad had been recruited he'd been singing songs about the subject. All his lost lovers were male anyhow, which somehow disgusted Milano. But for what they were paying him Conrad was good. Once he managed to put down his guitar he could pick up a gun and put it to good use.

It wasn't a gun that Conrad had to abandon his guitar for now though. Instead he opened up a briefcase and extracted from it an elaborate electronic device. Methodically he drew a long narrow antenna from it and then proceeded to drop it into the water. Into the control box he inserted a lead which was already connected to a small quartz clock. The time was 2:20.

Conrad and Milano now placed headphones over their ears and settled down on deck chairs to wait until they had their signal.

They didn't have long to wait. Eight minutes later a red light began to blink on the panel of the device. Conrad rotated the antenna in the water, clockwise, then counterclockwise. As he did so, the signal-strength meter fluctuated erratically. An expression of intense concentration came over Milano's face as he strained to interpret the sounds coming over the radio. Conrad's, by contrast, remained a perfect blank.

At last a smile gathered on Conrad's lips. "I've got it."

Milano listened a moment longer. "Yes, that's it."

Conrad fine-tuned the antenna to get it exact. "Eight miles, I'd say," Conrad muttered. "Maybe nine. And ten degrees to our right."

"Make it nine miles and ten degrees right," Milano affirmed.

Removing the headphones, Milano strode over to the helm. The pilot watched him impassively, anticipating the instructions.

Milano told him the speed he wanted the Cigarette taken in at.

"Fifteen minutes we should be in position, right in their path."

Milano had done these outings so often that he had the operation down to a science. He knew precisely how long these things required, how many minutes he should leave himself as insurance.

The thirty-foot powerboat assumed a southwesterly course that brought it to within three and a half miles of the *Confrontation*.

There the Cigarette stopped dead. Conrad brought up a signal beacon which he placed down on the bow. The beacon shot an amber light out on the water, which indicated that their craft was in distress. The *Confrontation* would be coming on them in another four minutes according to Milano's calculations.

Milano's calculations were right on the mark.

A pale yellow light on the northern horizon, followed shortly by the low rumble of Lehman-Ford diesel engines, heralded the immediate appearance of the *Confrontation*.

The Cigarette was so anchored that the larger boat would either have to stop or else alter its course if it was to avoid crashing directly into it.

As Milano hoped, the *Confrontation* began to slow, its motors dying to a muffled drone.

One man, then another, appeared on the port of the *Confrontation*, silhouettes in the glare of their deck lights.

"Ahoy there!" one of them called through a megaphone.

Milano popped into view in response. No one else was to be seen on the deck of the Cigarette.

"We need help!" Milano shouted back. "Out of fuel, food's running low. You think you have a little extra gas to get us going?"

"You hold on there."

117

"We're appreciative of whatever you can do."

Milano disappeared below deck for a moment. Conrad and the other two, Francis and the one who called himself Tennessee, were patiently whiling away the time until Milano issued them their orders. Close by their sides were the AKS rifles they relied on. The AKS was a recent Soviet addition to the burgeoning world of armaments, intended to replace that old favorite, the AK47 Kalashnikov. It had the advantage of being lighter and it fired a 5.54mm bullet with a hollow point and steel plug that slammed forward upon the bullet's impacting with the result that the bullet mushroomed, causing a much larger wound. The AKS was first tried out by Soviet troops against Afghan insurgents, but like all rifles, it made no distinction among targets. The crew of a yacht died as easily as Afghanis did once they were visited by a 5.54mm bullet.

The old man on the *Confrontation* was shouting back something now. Milano returned to the deck to see what he had decided.

"You got anything like a dinghy you can get over to us with? We have a few gallons we can give you. That should see you into port."

"No problem. We'll be over in a few minutes."

Conrad and Francis would be entrusted with the initial —and Milano hoped the final—assault. Milano would wait on the Cigarette with Tennessee as backup in case anything went wrong. But things hardly ever went wrong.

Milano deposited two packs of sugar in his coffee and stirred it inattentively while he watched the dinghy ease itself across the becalmed swath of water that separated the Cigarette from the Kong & Halverson Island Gypsy.

Because of his impatience and the state of his nerves, the short journey seemed to take an inordinate amount of time. But finally the dinghy came flush with the hull of the yacht. Francis, with Conrad right behind him, took hold of the rope ladder thrown to him and began clambering up to the deck. The canvas bags containing their weapons were slung unobtrusively over their backs.

Now all that remained for Milano to do was settle back and wait for the rattle of gunfire.

Slater Bodkin and Vincent appeared to welcome their guests on board. Two cans brimming full of gas rested at their feet.

Conrad nodded in greeting, Francis offered a smile that revealed a lot of gum and little teeth.

"Tell me, how'd you go and get yourself stuck out in the middle of the ocean like this?" There was no sarcasm in Slater's voice, he was just plain interested.

"Don't really know," Conrad said. "I know it sounds crazy but we strayed out farther than we expected. And something may be the matter with one of the tanks. Maybe sprung a leak."

Slater shook his head, wondering at such ignorance of the rudiments of sailing.

"Well," he said, gesturing toward the cans, "this should see you into the shore. By my reckoning there's a town about twenty miles due east of where we are now. You should be able to fuel up there with what you need."

Conrad nodded affably. "That's most kind of you. If you hadn't come along we might have been stuck out here for another day or two."

Francis regarded his companion uneasily. In an operation like this the object was to take the initiative and move fast. This desultory, meaningless conversation they were having only served to delay matters. Francis could not comprehend why Conrad was procrastinating in this manner. What he didn't realize was that Conrad was merely improvising a strategy on the spot. Something was troubling him, and he hoped to discover what it was before striking too precipitously.

"You don't mind if I use your head for a minute, do you?" Conrad addressed Slater.

"Go right ahead." Slater indicated the entrance to the cabin below deck. "Straight down and to your left."

Francis was not good with words. He hailed from Bolivia, but it wasn't a problem of not knowing English.

His Spanish was halting at best. So he set his body up against the gunwales and smiled his toothless grin at Slater, eyeing his canvas bag much too often. He was growing itchy, figuratively and literally. He kept on grinning stupidly and scratching his face and under his sweat-soaked arms. .

The albino meanwhile descended down into the cabin. No lights shown through from any of the staterooms. He assumed that the other crew members were asleep. Though it meant trusting Francis to act on his own without first alerting him to his plan, Conrad decided to seize the opportunity. He intended to eliminate all the opposition below deck in hope that Francis would do the same above.

To avoid the possibility of inadvertent discovery, he stepped inside the head, shut the door, and unzipped his canvas bag. From it he withdrew his AKS with its fresh clip.

Slipping quietly from the head, he approached the door to the master stateroom and cocked his ear to it. There was nothing to be heard. He threw open the door. Darkness greeted him. His rifle was targeted on the shadowy forms of the twin beds. But he refrained from firing for the simple reason that no one was occupying either bed.

He cursed, spun around, keeping the AKS extended. Two more doors remained to be opened, each leading to an aft stateroom.

When he was a child, Conrad had once heard a story about someone confronted with three doors. He didn't remember much of the story, but he did recall something about there being a treasure behind one of the doors, maybe two of them, but behind the third there were venomous snakes ready to spring. He wasn't exactly sure what the moral of this story was, but he had a strange feeling that he had become that character faced with the choices. And he couldn't help wondering which door would bring him luck and which the opposite.

He strained to hear what was going on on deck, but he heard nothing. Francis had not uttered a word to signal his presence.

Conrad knew he would have to act quickly now before the old skipper or his mate came down to see what was taking him so long.

No sense in deliberating as to whether the door on the left or the one on the right was the more auspicious choice. He chose the right.

And for his trouble got only more darkness.

And silence.

One door left, all other options used up.

Francis couldn't understand the reason for the delay. He feared that Conrad had fallen into a trap. He saw a hand reach out and muffle Conrad's mouth while a knife swept across his jugular

"Cigarette?" he asked. He wanted something to do with his hand besides put it to work scratching his fiery skin.

Vincent nodded, reached into his pocket and pulled out a pack of Salem's. He gave a cigarette to Francis and lit it for him. This distracted Francis long enough for Slater to seize hold of the canvas bag looped over his shoulder and to pull on it.

Slater, despite his advanced years, was strong enough to throw Francis off balance. In this brief interval Francis couldn't think of a proper response. Should he act outraged or try to get at his weapon?

"Let's see what you've got in there," Slater was saying, his voice deceptively soothing.

Vincent stepped within a foot of him, his eyes menacing.

Francis was stupid, that was something he himself would admit, but he was shrewd. He hadn't gotten this far without learning a few crucial lessons. So he decided to let the two men think they had the advantage.

"Señor wishes to see inside?" He maintained his moronic smile and hoisted the bag from his shoulder, setting it down on the deck. "Please go ahead, look."

When Vincent bent down to open it, Slater's eyes followed him. At that precise moment Francis slipped out his Bolo machete, a twenty-three-inch instrument with a steel blade that he kept sheathed inside his jacket.

Slater's eye caught the glint the blade made in the deck lights and instinctively ducked aside. Vincent turned to face him just as Francis brought the machete down. The blade sliced through the air, striking Vincent across the right shoulder but at such an angle that it slid across the bone rather than hacking into it. Nonetheless, it did succeed in tearing a great gash in Vincent's skin. Blood welled up instantly and soon covered Vincent's entire arm. "You fuck!" was Vincent's assessment of Francis' personality.

Francis, disturbed that he had managed to inflict such little damage, raised his machete again. Vincent and Slater had both backed off, but there was so little room on deck that they were virtually trapped.

But in the midst of his motion Francis abruptly stopped. The machete sailed out of his hands and thudded to the deck. Slater and Vincent studied him with immense curiosity as he stood there swaying back and forth, his hands busy trying to work the knife out of his back. It had come hurtling into him from the stern of the boat. It was a capable delivery. The knife had sunk in a few inches above his left kidney and almost to the hilt. There wasn't a great deal of blood yet because the knife was staunching the wound. But to Francis the most important thing in the world right now was to extricate the knife and return then to the business at hand. But it was difficult to get at the knife and all he was doing was enlarging the wound. And each time he tugged at the knife the pain it produced in him was so intense that he felt in danger of losing consciousness.

Now Max sauntered forward, abandoning his hiding place behind one of the bulkheads. He took his time. The pride he took in his marksmanship was evident on his face. He walked up to Francis with the air of someone who expected to engage in polite conversation and very deferentially said, "Let me do that." He then gently removed Francis' struggling hands from the bloody knife and pulled it straight out—all in one motion. He wasn't gentle. Francis gasped in pain and screamed out to his mother and God, both of whom had abandoned him long ago. Max, to shut him up, plunged the knife back into him—but in a different location this time just to add a little variety to the affair.

Francis no longer could summon the energy to scream. Rather he grunted with the onset of this new agony and sunk to his knees, his eyes rolling up in their sockets, showing the whites to the black sky. A stench rose up from him as his sphincter muscle involuntarily loosened. With one final shudder he toppled over, smacking his brow against the deck.

The albino meanwhile had yet to make a move. The AKS was still in his hands, but he felt himself paralyzed. He couldn't understand it, this had never happened to him before. He wanted to be back on board the Cigarette, playing his guitar.

He could not bring himself to open the door to the one remaining aft stateroom. Instead he opened fire, tearing a series of gaping holes in the door. Then he rushed in, expecting to find a body or two writhing on the floor. This did not turn out to be the case. No one was in this stateroom either.

In his disappointment he failed to notice the two men who emerged from out of the laundry room and utility closet respectively. But the sound of Booth's footsteps succeeded in alerting him. Booth was just naturally clumsy and loud. Nothing subtle about the man at all. It had been Booth's intention to slip up behind Conrad and perforate some vital part with the ten-inch combat knife he carried. This was Booth's nature. He liked to get close to his victims and dispatch them with a blade or hatchet or, failing that, his bare hands which were big, thick, and

123

calloused. But now he had no chance to take Conrad by surprise.

Conrad dropped to his knees and immediately let off a burst from the AKS. But because he'd been taken off guard his aim was wide of the mark. The clean wood paneling that lined the walls of the stateroom, however, received the injuries Conrad had intended for Booth.

Still, Booth reared back as though he had been shot, so great was his surprise. The problem was that he had no protection, nowhere to escape to. Conrad scrambled out of the empty aft stateroom and was all set to deliver a fatal round into Booth when Harry appeared and very calmly fired his Magnum.

Conrad had no time to reflect on this latest source of opposition, being too busy dying. With his fading consciousness he realized that in a single instant he had been hurtled all the way back into the aft stateroom, landing conveniently on one of the freshly made beds. The blood that sprung out of the wound in his back—which had begun in his upper abdomen—oozed into the spread, then soaked through the sheets and saturated the mattress. It would never wash out completely, that was obvious right off.

Like a talisman, the AKS remained fastened in Conrad's hands, but his grip was feeble and he could not make use of it much as he would have liked to. He thought once more of his guitar, and the image of an old lover to whom he'd addressed so many of his songs flashed into his mind in response. Then it was all gone, all gone. Conrad was not going to play guitar again.

Booth was still on the floor, hadn't quite consolidated himself to get himself off it yet, still psychologically being somehow prepared to have several rounds pumped into him. He stared up at Harry, more specifically at Harry's Magnum. It looked especially awesome at this angle. He had surmised that Harry was an agent of Keepnews, but Harry's possession of the Magnum and the facility with which he had employed it caused Booth to speculate over his mission anew.

Harry knew enough about human nature to realize that far from showing gratitude to him for saving his life, or even acknowledging that he had done so, Booth would hate him more fervently. Booth did not like to be put in such a humiliating position; he was not accustomed to it. And while he would respect Harry and Harry's powerful gun, he would nurture his hatred and one day, Harry was sure, manifest it in some particularly grim way.

But that was for another day. For now Booth said nothing, merely picked himself up from the floor and followed Harry up the steps to the deck which still stank of blood and feces and death. There Max was arguing with Slater about throwing Francis into the Pacific, an issue which Slater didn't want to be bothered with at the moment. He kept trying to rush below deck to see what had happened, but Max had grabbed hold of him, strangely unconcerned about Harry's fate or Booth's. What was of paramount importance in Max's mind was to dispose of Francis so that the deck could be cleansed of the godawful smell.

Vincent was paying attention to neither of these men. He was occupying himself in the pilothouse, bandaging the injury Francis' machete had caused him. When the gunfire sounded below deck he'd turned, crouching in the shadows, keeping an eye on the deck to see what the outcome of the conflict was. With the reappearance of Harry and Booth, he was satisfied he could escape a casual death this night.

But there was still the Cigarette anchored in the distance to deal with. Its allegedly fuelless engines came roaring to life and it turned on a course that would send it crashing into the *Confrontation*. Milano, having failed to receive radio confirmation that the yacht had been successfully captured, rightly assumed the worst. He still had Tennessee with him and the pilot, who was adequate with a gun when he didn't have to keep at the helm. If Milano had been wise he would have simply gone away. The powerboat was fast, and the *Confrontation* could never have caught up with it even if Slater had attempted to.

But Milano had never lost before, and it was not an idea he could get used to now. Hunkered down, he and Tennessee trained their AKSs on the yacht and opened fire even before they came in range, peppering the water about the *Confrontation*'s hull so that dozens of tiny geysers shot up everywhere.

Slater was desperately trying to lift anchor and guide his vessel out of the way of the advancing Cigarette. He was too involved in this operation to worry about the bullets that were now striking the boat itself, though still too low to do any damage. Occasionally, there'd be a nasty concussive sound that seemed to pierce the eardrums. Slater realized this was from the resistence offered by the bulletproof glass to the rounds impacting against it. Though the glass threatened to crack and in many instances was splintering, it did not give way completely. Which was fortunate for Slater since the pilothouse was partially wrapped in glass. Slater could have ducked down, he could have done this and still had a sufficient view of where he was going, but somehow he never considered it. It seemed right and proper to steer his boat fully erect and as confident as though this were just another normal outing.

There being only gunwales and no wall to use as a rampart, Harry had to lay flat out on the deck, hoping that the two men on the power boat would continue to fire at a sufficiently high trajectory, and in that way allow him to survive in good health.

Max and Booth were stretched out beside Harry, each firing 9mm semi-automatic carbines. Because of his injury, Vincent was incapable of using any sort of gun. Neither Max nor Booth had known until a few minutes before that the carbines—Mark 9s—were available at all. Only Harry and Slater were aware of their existence on board and Harry alone had known where they were hidden. But there was no question that Max and Booth were happy to get their hands on them rather than sitting out the battle.

More easily maneuverable, the Cigarette at the last

moment altered its course so that instead of ramming the *Confrontation* head-on, it turned sharply to the right, drawing alongside of it.

Harry sought to take out the pilot of the powerboat, but he lacked the opening he needed. All he could do was to keep the pilot pinned down in the cockpit. The fire was withering on both sides, but no one was scoring any hits. The situation threatened to persist indefinitely.

Desperate measures were called for. Slipping underneath the gunwales, Harry dropped down straight onto the deck of the powerboat. His action was so sudden, so unexpected, that neither Milano nor Tennessee had a chance to respond. Harry came down hard. The most immediate sensation he felt was a terrific stinging pain that set his whole left leg on fire.

But he ignored it—he had no choice—and rolling against the deck's wet and slippery surface, just avoiding a burst from Tennessee's AKS, he lifted his Magnum and fired. Having no time in which to sight his gun, he had to make do with shooting toward the stern, in the general direction of where he reckoned his antagonist to be.

He didn't do badly. The .44 caught Tennessee on his side, going clean through his shirt and taking with its passage a sliver of skin—not a large amount really, nothing that would cause serious injury—but certainly enough to create a great deal of pain, so much that Tennessee let out a shriek that might have awakened the sealife several fathoms below. He jerked up, forgetting that he was sacrificing his cover.

This allowed Booth or Max—whichever of the two had the better aim or better luck—to target him and bring him down. It seemed that at one moment Tennessee's head was there, whole and bristling with hair in every direction, and the next moment it wasn't; just turned a pulpous red with two horrified eyes staring out of it. Tennessee released another shriek, shriller than the last, and keeled over.

Milano, positioned behind a bulkhead was now in an unhappy predicament, having both Harry and the defenders on the yacht to contend with simultaneously. He called to the pilot, commanding him to speed the Cigarette out of the *Confrontation*'s range of fire. This way he would be able to reduce the scope of the conflict and the odds would be more in his favor.

The pilot heard Milano with no trouble, despite the fact that the door to the cockpit was closed. The Cigarette surged ahead, pulling away from the *Confrontation*. All Booth and Max could do was to send a few rounds in hapless pursuit of the vanishing boat. The water, and not the Cigarette, felt the brunt of their barrage.

Though his leg hurt like hell, Harry managed to maneuver himself back so that the starboard wall of the cockpit protected him. He flattened himself flush against it to minimize the exposed portion of his body.

Because Milano had deliberately doused the deck lights, darkness pervaded on the powerboat. This put Milano at a certain disadvantage because now he could not be certain where the invader had situated himself. And he did not intend to find out by risking his life. On the contrary, being of a practical bent, Milano decided that if necessary he would wait until it became light enough before making a move. He would stay right where he was. The pilot, if he knew what was good for him, would remain enclosed in the safety of his cockpit. Milano had no idea what the attacker wished to do, but he was convinced that he would have to do something—and shortly. Either reveal himself or else abandon the whole enterprise and jump off. Of course, if he did that then he would have to be a very good swimmer there being only a lot of Pacific ocean out there and not very much else. Except for sharks. There were, Milano figured, a great many of them.

There was no sound save the thrust of the engines and the splash of water as it yielded to the powerboat. Harry strained to keep his balance, every so often swinging his right leg back and forth, despite the pain this resulted in, just so that he could stop it from going numb. He was careful to keep silent, not wishing to give away his location. He began to sense, when he detected no movement on deck, what Milano had in mind. Dawn was approximately two and a half hours away but there would be a sufficient trickle of light before then to distinguish him from the obscurity.

So he decided he would crawl around to the bow which would give him more protection and might also allow him a chance at the pilot.

The pilot's face, visible through the glass, betrayed a look of intense concentration. His mouth was taut, his eyes fixed on the empty stretch of sea ahead of him. When he saw Harry making his way around the deck he slid the protective glass away so that he could fire the Smith and Wesson gripped in his free hand. The other was still locked on the wheel.

But Harry had anticipated this. He had brought only his head into view, providing for just enough temptation to impel the pilot to react. No sooner had he done this than he slipped back out of sight, just as the Smith and Wesson discharged.

All this happened so quickly that the pilot couldn't be sure whether he had hit Harry or not. It was conceivable he'd done so, and Harry had fallen straight into the sea. From the pilot's perspective it was impossible to tell. So he leaned out, poking his head into the wind to see just what had happened.

Which was when Harry, extending his Magnum out beyond the perimeter of the cockpit, answered his fire. Twice.

The first bullet slammed into the cockpit, just an inch or so above the pilot's head. This certainly would have provoked him into ducking back down had not the second shot smashed into his collarbone and partially deflected by the bone, continued at an upward trajectory into his throat, emerging out the back of his neck. The pilot was flung back, hitting the farthest wall before collapsing. The blood couldn't get out fast enough, it seemed, bursting simultaneously from the wound near his shoulder and from his open mouth.

Now Harry clambered up above the cockpit, resisting the impulse to cry out from the pain in his leg. After all, no matter how badly he felt, it was a whole lot better than the pilot did.

The powerboat was now under no one's control. It was heading at thirty knots per hour in a northeasterly direction and would continue to do so unless it ran aground or out of fuel.

Unquestionably, Milano had heard the exchange of fire, and it was quite likely he'd witnessed the slaying of the pilot. But of one thing there was no doubt—he had spotted Harry for he now loosened a barrage that swept right over Harry's body and out to sea.

But despite this attack Milano had lost one principal advantage: his hiding place. From his position on the roof Harry could see where Milano had attempted to conceal himself. He wasted no time in answering the fire from the AKS. The explosive force of the Magnum demolished a part of the bulkhead behind which Milano crouched. Fragments of wood belched up into the air. Some came raining down on Milano, and one particularly sharp fragment like a dagger dropped into his neck, piercing it for a depth of three inches. Blood erupted from the hole it gouged out in him. A cry of pain and shock followed immediately.

Milano grasped hold of the offending splinter, screaming, "Goddamn cocksucker, motherfucking son of a bitch!" though it was unclear whether he was referring to Harry who was responsible for the injury or to the wooden blade stuck in his neck. In any case, he was able to tug it all the way out, though this resulted in so much pain that he blacked out for several moments. When he opened his eyes again he saw Harry looming over him, the Magnum targeted on his head. What Harry had in mind was to ask Milano a few questions such as who hired him. But Milano, assuming that Harry meant to kill him directly without any formalities, decided he had nothing to lose and struggled to raise his weapon. Harry, of course, noted the movement and slammed his foot down on Milano's outstretched hand.

Milano winced at the pain that attacked him from this new location and wished Harry a quick death he seemed incapable of inflicting on him.

But rather than give up, with his free hand Milano grabbed hold of Harry's ankle and tried to throw him off balance. Now, ordinarily this would have accomplished nothing. Milano's grip wasn't strong enough and Harry's stance was such that he had gravity on his side. However, in this case, Milano was lucky enough to wrest hold of the leg that had been badly sprained when Harry first hit the deck.

The pain that shot up Harry's leg was sufficient to cause him to stumble. For a few critical seconds he lost his footing. As he sought to recover it, Milano seized the AKS and raised it to fire.

Harry, realizing his intention, quickly abandoned any notion of questioning him. Even though he had lost his balance he fired three times, exhausting his final clip of the night. Since he had no opportunity to take proper aim, he opted for the scattershot approach, figuring that he might get lucky too. If not, it was going to be some mean trick getting out of the way of a fusillade from an AKS.

But he needn't have worried. Through the smoke that filled the cool Pacific air with the stench of cordite he could make out the form of Milano. Or what was left of Milano. For all three bullets from the Magnum had entered and promptly gone through the man. The two wounds in his chest had merged by the time the bullets exited through the back so there was just one gaping hole beneath the shoulderblades from which bloody tissue was pouring out. The third wound had opened up Milano's abdomen, allowing his intestines to break free of the constraints his skin and muscles had imposed on them. The punch of the three successive shots had thrown

Milano as far as he could go across the deck. He was now propped up against the door of the cockpit. Weirdly, he was still alive. His glazed eyes fastened on Harry in a kind of wonderment. He seemed to be trying to get himself upright but could not succeed in doing so. Instead, he resigned himself to making a quiet exit from the world.

Harry hoisted him aside so he could get into the cockpit and then had to maneuver the lifeless pilot out of the way so that he could make it to the helm. This grim task completed, he began to turn the boat around, navigating it back from where it came in hope of finding the *Confrontation*.

He found her all right, though it took him a few hours. The sun was rising into the sky, heralding another hot summer day on the ocean by the time he came within sight of the yacht.

There was only one man on deck to witness his approach. Booth. He'd been swabbing the deck, presumably removing all the traces of blood Francis had gotten on it in his death throes. But now, seeing Harry, he put his mop down and picked up something else. It was only when Harry was less than twenty yards away that he saw what it was—one of the Mark 9s he'd used last night.

But this time he had it aimed on Harry. Harry was exposed and, what's more, was out of ammunition for the Magnum. Booth seemed to be debating with himself whether he should kill Harry, probably wondering whether he could get away with it. Or maybe he intended only to frighten Harry.

Harry, however, was too tired and wired-up to be frightened. Instead, he looked Booth in the eyes. Booth smiled, toying with the trigger. Then abruptly he put the carbine back down. For now there was someone else on deck—Max. And if murder was in Booth's heart, and it surely must be, it was too much of a private enterprise to proceed with it in front of a witness. Especially someone like Max who had proven so deft with a knife thrown from afar.

Max may not have noticed Booth's display of the Mark 9. If he had, he probably would have instigated a fight with him. It didn't require much to provoke Max, after all.

But right at this moment Harry was certainly pleased to see him. Max's timely appearance might have saved his life. In any case, Max now stepped up to the starboard side of the boat and in a surprising show of politeness actually waved to Harry in greeting.

"Thought we'd lost you!" he shouted out.

"Not yet," Harry replied. "Not yet."

Chapter Fourteen

An early morning mist shrouded Carangas from view. Along the coast as far as the eye could see the palms and the wild tropical plants that grew cheek to cheek with them dripped with moisture. Birds cawed and hooted in the stillness. As the *Confrontation* approached the shore, the water turned increasingly brackish. A sweet, putrifying smell rose up from the dense foliage and carried out on the humid air.

No one, not Booth, not Max nor Vincent, had asked why Carangas was their destination. They were crewmen, hired only to get Keepnews' boat to where its skipper wished it to go. But standing on the deck, viewing the apparently inhospitable landscape, they seemed none too pleased. "What's here in this fucking place?" Vincent inquired, but the question was clearly rhetorical.

Slater was busy examining the charts, trying to ascertain where they could best anchor. "It gets shallow from this point on. Chance of running aground," he said to Harry, jabbing a bruised finger on the most detailed chart. "It looks like we'll have to use the skiff to get on shore."

With one eye on the depth sounder, Slater carefully navigated the yacht south and then in toward where the chart indicated Carangas should be. He could acquire no independent confirmation with his eyes alone because the mist was still too thick.

To supplement the depth readings he switched on the Micrologic-220, which he used to measure how much he might be deviating from the course he'd plotted for himself. The readouts allowed him to see how many microseconds either right or left of course he was; it further told him how much time remained, if maintaining present speed, before he reached his destination. Present speed wasn't much. The vessel was proceeding at a speed that could only be called ridiculous.

In addition, Slater relied on a Mariner 2600 with a radome-enclosed antenna/receiver, which he used as a back-up radar system. The display unit could, with accuracy, register up to twenty-four miles. The luminous scope revealed that there was considerable activity in the vicinity even though they could see nothing. Six, then seven other boats appeared as shadowy forms on the screen, heading into shore or away from it. But only one point on shore mattered—Carangas. The digital readout showed that they were within ten minutes of attaining the town.

Harry turned on the VHF radio, dialing past the international weather stations, not quite certain what he was searching for as he scanned the frequencies. Occasionally he would monitor an exchange in rapid-fire Spanish. More often he would find himself listening to a sequence of beeps and high-pitched whines that sounded no more intelligible than the calls the birds were making in the lush vegetation.

Though there was a SSB radio—single sideband—it made no sense to try that. It was a more complex system, but it was useful only for a range greater than the thirty miles the VHF was capable of receiving from.

As the *Confrontation* penetrated the heavy gray atmosphere certain objects, previously hidden, began to emerge. Off to the port side the crew could make out a small pleasure cruiser, but it was positioned awkwardly, and when they came closer they could see why. It had been cast up against a huge rock that protruded abruptly from the murky waters. The bottom of the hull was visible; the rudder was half broken off and rusted. Seaweed clustered thickly about the abandoned craft.

It became obvious that this boat had not simply run aground in a squall or as a result of careless navigation. Gouged out of the hull and the windows of the helm station were several holes that could only have been produced by bullets. What could have been dried blood—it was now a dull brownish stain—obscured one of the windows entirely from view.

Though no one spoke the same thought entered the minds of all the crewmen: Why Carangas?

Suddenly the yacht's engines shuddered and stopped dead. The anchor was unwound and dropped to the bottom.

Presently Slater appeared. "Well," he said almost apologetically, "we seem to be here."

"Here?" Vincent gazed around him with incredulity. "Here? What the fuck are you talking about?" He regarded Slater as though he'd taken leave of his senses.

"Sorry, it all checks out. The charts, the radar. We are half a mile off shore." He gestured vaguely to his left, beyond the stricken pleasure cruiser. "Unless the maps are wrong Carangas should be over there. Generally in a situation like this what I'd suggest we do is just rest a while till the sun comes along and burns some of this shit away."

"I don't like it here," mumbled Booth, studying the pleasure cruiser, with its seaweed and bullet holes left like souvenirs. "I think this is shit." He turned to Harry, and not to Slater, correctly surmising that it was Harry who would know the answer, "How long we going to be here?"

"Not long," Harry said. Because the fact was he wasn't especially pleased about the prospect of going into

Carangas. The prospect of remaining there any length of time seemed to him a fatal one. He did not expect either a traveler's information service or a friendly hotel to put them up. And he didn't care to speculate as to what the guided tours would be like. He began to get a good idea why this was a drug runner's paradise.

"Not long" was not a reply that Booth liked. Under his breath he cursed Harry, as he'd been doing since they left San Francisco. He was, however, having trouble breathing fresh life into these old curses. He'd run through every one he knew (and there were a great many after being at sea for years) and contrived all sorts of variations, but somehow none of them seemed quite suitable to express his distaste for Harry. After Harry had saved his life, a fact he refused adamantly to admit to himself, he had transferred just about all of his hatred from Max to the former Inspector #71. He did not know anything regarding Harry's background; that would have only fueled the hatred all the more.

It did not happen slowly. No, all at once the mist was dispelled, burning away with so much speed that it reminded Harry of a woman breathlessly flinging her garments aside, exposing herself in the full beauty of her nakedness. Not just any woman. Wendy, specifically. He was surprised by the force of the memory. He had not thought of her since they'd started out, in fact, had felt grateful to escape her and her mad schemes to betray her husband. But now he would like to be with her and leave behind these violent crewmen, at least two of whom nurtured the desire to kill him.

A brilliant sun, blisteringly hot, shone down from the east, bleaching the sky, softening the putrid green hue of the water below to a color slightly more palatable.

And there became visible in this sudden light the town of Carangas. Amid palm and banana and mango trees, a honeycomb of white edifices, with walls of adobe and stucco, could be discerned. None of the structures, save one, was over two stories tall. A ramshackle wharf protruded into the water. To either side of it were tied half a dozen launches and rowboats, the latter presumably used by the villagers when they went out to meet arriving vessels. Even this early in the morning, and it was only a few minutes past the hour of six, you could hear the town coming to life: the squawks of chickens and insistent crowing of cocks and the cries of children and the harsh voices of their mothers urging them into the day.

On the face of it, there was nothing to indicate that this was any different from all the other small coastal towns that dotted the shoreline of the Pacific all the way south to Tierra del Fuego. To all appearances it could be the bananas that grew on the surrounding trees that constituted Carangas' principal export and not heroin. But thinking back to the stabbing death of Chuck Loomis, Harry realized he had dramatic confirmation that this was the place he was looking for. And certainly that disabled bullet-riddled cruiser testified to the violence that, even if hidden during the day, no doubt came out in full force at night.

Actually, it wasn't what you'd call exactly hidden in the day either. As their skiff tied up at the wharf, several interested citizens appeared to scrutinize the visitors. They were all armed. They made no effort to conceal the guns that rested on their hips or the large knives sheathed in leather. Only one was clean-shaven; the others sported mustaches and beards, and as though all this hair did not dominate their faces enough, they also went in big for sunglasses that obscured not only their doubtless bloodshot eyes but a good portion of their cheeks as well. The result was you didn't get to see very much of their faces and nothing at all of their expressions.

You could see their teeth when they smiled, but their smiles were cryptic; it was unlikely these smiles were intended to welcome the newcomers. Instead they suggested malevolence and the joyous anticipation of impending bloodletting.

No one came up to them to ask for their papers. Instead, a small boy whose eyes seemed much too old and experienced popped out of nowhere and throwing his

137

arms open, proposed in acceptable English that they stay at the Posada de los Candiles, which he proceeded to point out to them. It was the two-story structure they had spotted from the boat. On the upper floor a buxom woman of indeterminate age was draping a dusty rug over the grilled railing of the terrace. "Get out of the way, you filthy little bugger," Booth said, blocking the kid's way. "Probably carrying some fucking disease."

Booth was not the sort to try and get to know the natives.

Vincent, however, thought that maybe the boy could be of use.

"You direct us to the local gin mill? Taverna? Bar-grill?" He ran out of Spanish words real quickly.

The boy was delighted to be of help. "Si, si, you come with me. Bar-grill taverna, si, come, come."

Slater and Harry hung back, allowing Booth and Vincent to explore what little in the way of leisurely pursuits Carangas had to offer. They were instructed to be back on board the *Confrontation* by eleven that night. Max, meanwhile, was on the boat, guarding it.

Harry did not wish to involve anyone else in his surveillance, certainly not Vincent, Booth, or Max, none of whom he trusted. But Slater, aware more by intuition than by what had thus far been disclosed to him of what Harry was up to, grew insistent. "An old man like me, he's seen a lot of things over the years, done some number of things too, but I am not one to retire on my memories. Even when you get my age you need a little adventure now and then."

"I would have thought that after that battle we had on the high seas you would have had all the adventure you wanted."

Slater threw his head back laughing. "Ah no, Harry, there you're wrong. All that did was whet my appetite for more."

Harry explained to Slater that his first objective was to discover what he could about the heroin operation that

138

had its base here and then to find out what he could about the security the refiners and drug runners employed. And that was practically all he reasonably could hope to do. If, in addition, he could also ascertain how the piracy was conducted, and who was instrumental in planning it, why that would be a bonus. What Keepnews would do with this information, whether he would assemble a small army and invade Carangas (and he was certainly capable of doing something like that), or whether he would have already lost interest in this mission (and that was not to be completely unexpected), Harry had no idea.

The one thing that Harry hoped not to have to do was become entangled with the men who were involved in this business. And from the looks of things, just about everybody in town was.

After further enlightening Slater about some of the more cogent details of Keepnews' assignment, Harry waited for him to react, almost hoping that he had sufficiently discouraged the aging skipper from continuing on with him.

But Slater refused to go anywhere. "I figured that it might be something like that. I don't know why Harold didn't tell me in the beginning. I can hold a secret well as the next man. Better in fact. But it's not important now. So how are we going to do this?"

They were standing at the beginning of Calle Aurora, which was a pretty name for an ugly street whose pavement had crumbled years before, allowing weeds and sand to break through. The high stone walls that lined both sides of this narrow street were covered with political graffiti—hammers and sickles in bright red paint and slogans that espoused one political confederation or the other. Calls for revolution seemed to be a big thing in this town. The deposited urine and shit—burro shit and human shit—gave the atmosphere an especially fetid odor.

"So how are we going to do this?" Slater repeated. You

could tell he was becoming excited by the way his teeth kept chopping down on the well-notched stem of his pipe.

"We make like buyers. We are looking for high-priced heroin. Maybe a kilo now and a few kilos later to be picked up on another occasion."

Slater gave Harry a cursory inspection. "You could do it. You look like someone with money to blow."

"I suppose that's a compliment. Now for the first time I believe we are fortunate in having Booth and Vincent with us. They would impress a dealer as boys so despicable and ruthless and untrustworthy that they could not be involved in anything else but drugs. They're a good cover for us. It's just the idea of taking them back that gets me."

"Ah, but look, Harry, they did their jobs. They got us down here with no trouble. It's in their natures to squabble now and again."

Harry shot a sidelong glance at Slater. He liked Slater well enough, but he sometimes couldn't help thinking that the man was going a bit senile. Harry's definition of a squabble did not include putting knives to one another's throat.

But rather than say anything further Harry directed Slater down Calle Aurora. He had no particular destination in mind—Carangas wasn't so big that you couldn't walk through the whole town in half an hour. He assumed that eventually he would come across a main plaza. The important thing was that their progress should be observed and their interest in being in Carangas correctly measured. Sooner or later he reasoned someone would turn up with an intriguing proposition for them.

True to Harry's expectations, a man was following them, a short homely son of a bitch with a snaggly-toothed grin and the unhappy posture of a hunchback. At first Harry believed he was simply a beggar, but it became apparent that if this were true, he was doing a lousy job of it. He kept well behind them. His only purpose seemed to be to remind them he was there.

As Calle Aurora trickled into Av. el Cortez, another man materialized. He also was short but plumper than the first, and his eyes bore the look Harry generally associated with an addled mind. His lips had similarly played into a moronic grin that was beginning to seem like the town's dubious trademark.

On Calle Los Cocos, which ran directly into a market where women fondled bloody hunks of unidentifiable meat and harangued the butchers, yet another man appeared. He was not just lean but skinny, and his flesh was liberally sprinkled with strange nauseating eruptions. Just looking at him was enough to make you feel as though you'd been contaminated. He, with an absolutely impassive expression on his face (no grin this time), joined the other two in tracing Harry and Slater's meandering path.

"This is getting to be some kind of freak show," Harry remarked, wondering whether the gene pool of the town had been visited by some diabolical curse. Inbreeding was a more likely explanation: preserve everybody's worst traits and pass them to the next generation.

Though none of these three specimens looked to be armed, their halting walks, their disfigurements, and their unworldly expressions caused Harry to become more queasy than if they had been bearing guns. Slater seemed somewhat oblivious to their presence, but it was clear that he was aware of them. His lips were pursed and he was uncharacteristically silent.

The market, however, was not. The women who congregated there were shouting like banshees in their feverish bargaining over prices. Flies whirled madly about the cuts of goat and lamb that hung from the stalls. The air was rank with the smell of Carangas, a smell composed of rot and running blood.

This is a place, Harry thought, where reason wasn't just asleep. Somebody had killed it off and buried it in an unmarked grave.

The three creatures were still behind them. One was way over to their left, another to their right, and one just sort of hovered about, always careful to maintain a respectable distance. Even in the tumult of the market, with its narrow lanes strewn with crushed vegetables and over-rippened fruit, they could not succeed in throwing them off their path. And actually Harry recognized the futility of trying to do so. In Carangas it was impossible to escape attention for long, especially if you stuck out as Harry and Slater did, even if that had been their objective.

Emerging from the market, their shadows following them out along with the rancid smell, Harry and Slater discovered that they had now come upon the plaza, in this case, the Plaza del Sol. It wasn't much of a sight to see though. There was a small park dead in the middle of it and a crumbling fountain that failed to jettison any water into the air and a cluster of vendors and shoeshine boys who appeared too stunned by the intensity of the heat to bother selling their wares even to these gringos.

Perhaps it was not the heat after all. Perhaps it was the presence of the three freaks who dogged their tracks and in that way made it clear to the demoralized citizenry of Carangas that neither Harry nor Slater were to be disturbed.

This second possibility seemed to be borne out within minutes when a bespectacled man, wearing a white jacket and white slacks, stepped into their path and with deferential reserve addressed them both. "You are Americans, yes?"

He appeared to be enjoying the last years of his seventh decade. His skin was leathery and dark but there was a strange shimmer to it, a gloss, as though he'd been baked in a kiln for half his life. His frame was small, and his hands had smooth long fingers with nails that had obviously been manicured.

"That's what we are all right," Slater answered. "True-blood Americans."

"My name is Ignacio Mendoza, and since we so seldom find visitors in our town I would be delighted to invite you to have a drink with me."

"We'd be honored," Harry said.

142

Ignacio reached out to grip his hand, then Slater's. Harry declared that his name was Peter Williams which was the first thing that came to mind. Slater looked momentarily confused, then understanding the need for an alias assumed one of his own: "Mac Watson."

"It is a great pleasure, Mr. Williams, Mr. Watson."

Ignacio's voice betrayed his suspicion that these were not their true names, but it was also evident that true names were not what was expected in a place like Carangas.

Ignacio insisted that they all have whiskey, being under the impression that all gringos preferred whiskey to anything else. He did not want to be disillusioned in this respect.

The cafe where they were sitting fronted out on the plaza. The cafe was called Mixteca, and it seemed to be inhabited chiefly by dissolute-looking characters who busied themselves smoothing their bristling mustaches with their hands.

Out on the plaza, in the shade of a palm whose fronds had been fried to a crisp by the unrelenting sun, stood the three sideshow escapees, each one indolently watching Harry and Slater as Ignacio maneuvered the conversation away from comments on the weather and the tortured state of Mexico City politics to a subject of far more reaching importance—at least to Ignacio.

"Tell me, gentlemen," he said, his voice crisp as an autumn day in New England and just barely touched by an accent, "would you be interested in discussing a business venture?"

"What kind of business venture you got in mind?" Slater took his cue automatically.

"A venture that could make you a considerable amount of money and one that entails minimal risk."

"I expect you would be profiting from it," said Harry.

Ignacio laughed. "Naturally. Myself and my partners. You have, I expect, brought an interesting sum of money to Carangas."

"Interesting?" Harry pressed.

"Well, gentlemen, we do deal only in certain minimum

143

quantities. It would not make sense to consider business transactions that are not tied to interesting sums of money." He liked that phrase and was going to stick firmly to it.

"We understand completely," Harry assured him. "I assume you take American Express."

Perhaps because Harry kept a straight face, Ignacio failed for a moment to realize that this was a joke. Then, suddenly understanding, he broke into laughter, nearly doubling over. "You gringos!" he said. "What a strange sense of humor you have. American Express! I think this is madness on your part." Wiping his eyes free of tears, he regained his composure. "So then you will come along and meet my partner." It was not a question.

"Is he far from here?"

"Not so far. But we must go by a jeep. The road is a difficult one."

Ignacio stood up and motioned to the hunchbacked man who waited beneath the burnt-out palm. He quickly disappeared from sight but more quickly reappeared, navigating a Land Rover onto the plaza.

Slater drew Harry off to the side, taking advantage of Ignacio's distraction. "Tell me something, you have all that much money to make a buy if you have to?"

"Frankly, all I've got on me is about thirty dollars."

"More than I have. You don't generally get very much for money like that. Especially if what you're buying is a large quantity of high-grade heroin."

"You have a point there," Harry said thoughtfully.

Slater wondered at his calmness. "You thinking we can stall them? Convince them we'll get the money to them later?"

Ignacio turned toward them, curious to see whether they were coming or not. Slater gave him a wide smile. "Be right there!" he called.

"Let's hope we can," Harry said.

"Otherwise?"

"Otherwise . . . . otherwise we're in big trouble."

The little boy who offered Booth and Vincent directions to a local cantina seemed infinitely resourceful. Not only did he inform the two insolent Americans where they could acquire a prostitute, or several if they preferred, a virgin (who was, naturally, reputed to be his sister), but he also recommended a local pusher to him—an "amigo" —who could supply them with every conceivable drug— uppers, downers, heroin, cocaine, hashish, marijuana, etc. "One day I go to America!" he proudly proclaimed to them, though he neglected to say whether he would bring all his illicit wares with him when he went.

While Vincent responded favorably to the idea of experimenting with one of the local ladies, Booth was far less enthusiastic, recalling the many times he'd contracted the clap from whores in similar ports. But the prospect of throwing some intriguing chemical down their throats (or inhaling or injecting it, however they had to do it) inspired them both.

Los Cocos was the name of the cantina to which the kid guided them, always keeping a few steps ahead, repeatedly urging them on as though he expected at any moment to lose his customers.

Los Cocos was a dreary establishment. Even at midday it was half-occupied, mostly by the unemployed and unemployables of the town, but also by foreigners, Americans among them, who all called themselves importers without necessarily adding that it was heroin they imported. They had an air of self-importance about them, but they were obviously bored. There was no action, only mescal, pulque, and tequila, and the maddening monotonous songs that emerged from an old Zenith portable radio. A part of the wall-length mirror behind the bar was pockmarked and cracked. You would not have to be an expert to see that the damage had been done by bullets, probably fired by someone who'd gotten too loaded or too tired of waiting for a connection.

The boy even felt compelled to shepherd them to a particular table. No one paid the new arrivals much attention. They were too used to new arrivals in this cantina. "Mescal yes, you wish mescal?" The boy would have been displeased had the men wished anything else. But in fact mescal was what they were both looking forward to.

Accommodatingly, the boy brought them mescal, then vanished with the speed of a poltergeist off to do more mischief.

"Where did the fucker go?" Booth asked.

"To get his fucking amigo, I suppose."

Vincent was on target. Within five minutes, the amigo in question arrived. He looked quite stoned on whatever it was he was plying; his eyes were dilated, but he barely appeared to be seeing anything with them. A handlebar mustache virtually hid his lips from view. A cowlick dropped down over his brow and a big white theatrical sombrero submerged his whole face in shadow.

"What a winner we got," Booth noted, staring at the man who came up to their table, nodding his head deferentially while he introduced himself as Garcia something —neither Booth nor Vincent could catch his Christian name.

The boy of course wouldn't go away until he'd been adequately compensated for his many services of the day. Vincent stuffed a few pesetas in his hand. The boy glanced down to see just how much it was and looked back up, gazing miserably at his benefactor. "Not enough!" he protested.

"Plenty enough!" shouted Garcia, who didn't want his business dealings disrupted. He slapped his open hand against the boy's face, turning half of it bright scarlet. The boy was flung back by the force of the blow. In Spanish he screamed an imprecation at the three of them and scampered from the cantina before he incurred further injury.

"Now we talk business!" Garcia said happily. Leaning toward the two gringos with a conspiratorial glimmer in his otherwise deadened eyes, he said, "You come on the boat this morning?"

Vincent owned that they had.

"You go back soon?"

Vincent said he was sure their stay wouldn't be very long.

"You wish to make mucho money for yourselves?"

Vincent slugged down his glass of mescal. Booth replied for the two of them. "That's always an interesting proposition."

"You would like to transport something for me? You bring it to California, to maybe San Francisco?"

Neither man saw fit to question him as to how he had surmised their ultimate destination.

"Could be," Booth muttered, warily regarding the man. He too needed additional mescal if he were to cope with this situation.

More mescal was then brought to them.

"You could, I think, take back for me three, maybe four kilos of shit?" He used shit not as a scatalogical curse, but as a word upon which he conferred great respect. It was just that he was so accustomed to employing it in this context that no other synonym jumped readily to mind.

"Nice try, baby," Vincent said, "but you're out of our league. We ain't got that kind of bread."

Garcia knitted his brow. "What do you mean talking like this? What do you need bread for?"

Vincent and Booth exchanged a puzzled glance. They concluded that Garcia was quite obviously deranged and that there was no sense in listening to him further.

But Garcia had an entirely plausible explanation. "We will pay you for delivering a consignment."

"Oh?" Vincent believed that he, much more than Booth, was capable of conducting these negotiations. "And why should you trust us?"

Garcia's smile was appropriately enigmatic. "We do not make such offers lightly. We are well aware of who you are and why you are here."

"That's more than anyone's told us," Booth noted bitterly.

"And, as you can imagine, if you do not make the delivery your lives would be worthless."

Without needing to inquire who was behind Garcia, the two gringos recognized the truth of his words.

"How much money would we be getting?" Vincent asked, hastening to specify, "each?"

"Ah, then you are interested." Garcia clapped Vincent on the shoulder as though he'd made a very wise decision. "Before we begin such talk, señors, why don't we go to my house? It is not far from here, and there you can also have a taste of what you will be bringing to America. Unless that does not suit you."

"No, no," Booth assured him, "that suits the fuck out of us."

Chapter Fifteen

Hidden by organ cacti, by cacti too obscure to have ever been named by humankind, by soapweed and lantana, by passion flowers, marigolds, by banana and date trees and by palms, the Villa Corona could barely be seen, just the glimmer of a high white stucco wall emerging from all this lush and hideous vegetation.

The rutted, dusty road that led fifteen kilometers from Carangas now narrowed so much so that it could barely accommodate the Land Rover. Then it wound down into a declivity, through the dense foliage which gave off a scent so ripely sweet that it was almost cloying, coming at last to a gate that looked to be unguarded. It was not, however, as Harry discerned. There were two palm trees on either side of the gate and protruding inconspicuously from each was the eye of a video camera which swung slowly from side to side, scanning the immediate area. There was no question in his mind that there were other monitors close by.

Patiently, and without offering any explanation, Ignacio waited, and beside him the hunchbacked creature clung to the wheel, his eyes bright with the anticipation of getting the durable jeep in motion again.

At length a man appeared—no freak but someone in excellent health and full command of his faculties. He wore no uniform but he was armed, an AKS hugged to his chest, a .45 on his hip. With a nod of recognition he drew open the gate and allowed the Land Rover to pass through.

The villa, like a mirage, kept appearing through the trees, but because of the way in which the road wound, looping circuitously, it never seemed quite attainable.

Birds squawked, perhaps to signal the coming of the men in the Land Rover, but otherwise there was no sign of sentient life, human or otherwise. Of the sky there was practically nothing to see because of the way the forest grew, roofing them over with leaves and fronds, blotting out all but an occasional burst of light when the afternoon sun could penetrate.

Finally, they arrived at the Villa Corona. It was not nearly so big or impressive as Harry had imagined it. Nonetheless, it was a lovely structure, all of white but trimmed along its sides and around its several square windows with a subdued orange. At the door, also orange in color, stood a second guard, shooing away preying mosquitoes with his hands. Seeing Ignacio, he shot up to attention, then unlatched the door so the party could enter.

Though the vestibule into which they walked was dark and quiet, empty save for the presence of some ancient cracked urns, it was obvious that activity was occurring elsewhere. Men's voices could be heard and the sound of footsteps across mud-baked floors. All this noise seemed to be coming from below them.

"Come with me, gentlemen, I wish to introduce you to my partner."

Ignacio's partner had not expected company, that was clear from the onset. A buxom girl in a peasant dress and a lowcut white blouse that seemed unequal to the task of constraining her top-heavy breasts sat giggling on his lap, permitting him as many liberties as he chose to take and they were a great many. One enormous hand, scarred white along the palm where he had managed to stop the progress of a knife into his heart, had dug itself down below the white fabric to cup the left breast, which was struggling to emerge. The other, distinguished by the lack of three middle fingers that had been sacrificed in yet another battle, was feverishly tracing the rounded contours of her thigh, in the process causing her long embroidered dress to hike up way above her knees.

Ignacio did not seem at all perturbed at this public display, nor did his partner, whom he had yet to introduce, seem at all conscious that he now had an audience. Maybe he wanted an audience. The Mexican girl, however, did take notice of the intruders, but this only caused her to giggle harder.

"Meet my partner, Señor José Virgilio."

José Virgilio's massive head appeared from behind the tangle of female hair that had kept it hidden and a great enthusiastic smile revealed a full set of teeth that had all been capped in gold. To look at his teeth was like staring a flashbulb in the face when it popped off.

Of Virgilio's eyes, only one seemed to be functioning. The other was mostly empty, a bloody white that lacked a pupil. The sight of him so startled Slater that he abruptly turned his head away.

Virgilio evidently was quite aware of the effect he had. He let out a bitter laugh, gave a tug to his slight obtuse triangle of a beard, and unceremoniously pushed the girl from his lap, sending her tumbling to the floor. Slapping her soundly on the rump was sufficient to propel her screaming out of the room.

Seizing Slater's hand, then Harry's, Virgilio greeted them. He did not wait for Ignacio to introduce them. There was no necessity of that. He already knew what their names were—not the aliases they had assumed in the plaza but their true names.

Harry, still trying to maintain the forced spirit of cordiality that Ignacio had instituted, nearly froze to hear his name and Slater's pronounced by this man whom neither of them had ever heard of before, much less met. The thought struck him with terrifying immediacy that they had been set up. If their identities were known at the Villa Corona, then it was likely that their purpose in coming to Carangas was similarly known.

"So you have come to purchase our heroin?" Virgilio inquired, a false heartiness in his voice. "We already have many buyers, you understand, but we can always use more. To heroin there is no end. The poppies flourish, the farmers grow wealthy. Why should there not be more heroin?" He turned, pushing his monstrous face into Slater's. "I speak extraordinary good English, don't I?"

Slater regarded him with distaste but nodded all the same.

"That is because I lived in your country and studied there. At San Francisco State College, you know of it? My parents, God keep their souls, had a great deal of money so that they could afford to send me to the States. We should all have so much money, no?"

Now he held up his nearly digitless hand, proudly exhibiting the stumps where there used to be full fingers. "Understand that I did things that my education did not intend me to do. My parents, God keep their souls, were disappointed in me. But I had a temper, no? And much ambition." He fixed his eyes on Harry. "And you too have much ambition." He tilted his head, a feigned expression of deep sorrow came upon his face. "And it is disappointing that you shall end your life without ever being able to fulfill your ambition. It is also a shame that it has fallen upon me to deprive you of living out your allotted time."

Harry said nothing to this, would not lower his eyes or avert them from his would-be executioner. Slater's hands were trembling, but he seemed determined to retain his dignity. Ignacio, on the other hand, appeared immensely pleased at the ease with which he had succeeded in trapping his quarry.

"You though," Virgilio spoke now to Slater, "you would seem to have so little time left that your death will be almost a formality."

"You disgust me," Slater muttered. His voice was scratchy, labored, betraying his extreme nervousness.

Harry regretted that he had permitted Slater to accompany him, but he had not believed that the danger would be so immense. "How did you know who we were?"

"How did we know?" Virgilio thought that this must be a joke. He began laughing. Ignacio thought this rather humorous himself and joined in the laughter.

"We have a friend in San Francisco," said Ignacio patiently, "and he took pains to inform us that you would be coming here."

"Friend?" Harry had an idea who the friend might be.

"He is called, I believe, Father Nick."

Father Nick had somehow managed to get his revenge even in this remote unmapped place.

But what Harry could not comprehend was how Father Nick had discovered the mission he was undertaking on behalf of Harold Keepnews. No matter how he ran it over in his mind it didn't jibe.

Virgilio, unlike his minions, did not appear to be armed. And from what Harry could see, neither was Ignacio. Nonetheless, action, even desperate action, was out of the question. While he hadn't been frisked and was still in possession of the Magnum and a much smaller .22 strapped to his ankle and hidden under his pants leg, to produce either of them now would be, he knew, utter folly. For without needing to turn around he realized he and Slater were being carefully watched by some of the same armed men they had seen earlier. Virgilio was not the sort of a man to expose himself unnecessarily to risk despite the testimony of his battered flesh.

"We shall commit your souls to God—that is if He is prepared to receive you—very soon. Only not here. This is my home and place of business. My laboratories are situated in the basement. My workers are coming and going all the time. They are peaceful men, concerned only with distillation and refining. I would not wish them to think me inhospitable to my guests. So you shall both be executed outside, away from here. With these temperatures, with such humidity, you will be surprised at how quickly your bodies will putrify and be swallowed up by the plants."

Soundlessly, three men, all wearing dull white tunics, all brandishing Karl Gustav submachine guns, appeared, stepping up behind Harry and Slater in response to Virgilio's command.

"You will forgive me," Virgilio addressed them, "if I do not see you to the door. It is a dereliction of my responsibility as host, I know, but I have other obligations that demand my attention."

One of those obligations, Harry surmised, was undoubtedly the buxom peasant girl.

"You will please surrender your weapons," Ignacio said, reminding his partner that this rather important detail had been neglected.

Harry threw down his .44 which landed with a jarringly loud clunk against the tiled floor. He did nothing to draw attention to the .22 strapped to his ankle.

One of the guards now poked his weapon against Slater's back, grunting to make his—and the gun's—point clearer. He had evidently decided that Slater must also be armed, and he wasn't going to be satisfied until he had confirmation of this fact.

Slater turned swiftly, angrily, toward the man and without considering the consequences, slapped him across the face with the back of his hand. This took everyone by surprise, and for a moment no one, not even the offended guard, reacted.

There was a moment of dead silence in the room. Then the guard lunged forward, hoping to deliver a more painful injury to Slater with the butt of his gun. Slater, proving astonishingly agile for someone his age, managed to avoid the blow and the weapon simply glanced off the side of his arm. This man's difficulties in subduing Slater were clearly amusing his companions and even Virgilio and Ignacio, for they made no move to aid him. Instead they stood right where they were, laughing, waiting for an entertaining climax.

Something seemed to have come unhinged in Slater. Faced with imminent death, he appeared to gain rather than lose confidence. His eyes were inflamed, his gray hair stuck out wildly from his pink, sunburned scalp. "This what you're after, you son of a bitch?" he challenged his assailant.

Harry looked to see him holding up a knife that was ordinarily employed to cut bait and filet tuna. It was stained and not as sharp as it might have been, but it was effective for all that. Harry had not known he'd been carrying it and could not quite understand how he had gotten it out so quickly. It might well have been sleight of hand: the rabbit plucked out of the hat.

This changed everything of course, but no one in the room could actually believe Slater would use the knife, Harry included. Indeed, the entertainment value of the proceedings seemed only to have increased. The smiles that had perched on the lips of the men remained where they were.

Harry realized now that all eyes were turned on Slater and the determined guard and that the .44 lay unobserved only half a foot away from him. It was possible that Slater hadn't gone mad after all, that he was doing his utmost to provide the distraction necessary for Harry to recover his weapon.

But at that moment Harry still could not risk even the slightest movement without drawing attention back to himself.

The guard said something unintelligible to Slater, presumably urging him to drop the knife. But far from dropping it Slater was whipping it through the air, daring the Mexican to advance closer. There was no question that the guard was so frustrated now that he would have simply liked to shoot Slater and be done with it. But he knew that this would be a violation of orders and would, besides, cut short the little drama that his employers found so highly amusing.

So he had to make do with clubbing Slater senseless or else ramming him directly, which was the alternative he chose, charging in at him like a bull ready to gore a particularly brazen matador. His thinking in this strategy wasn't exactly coherent. For one thing, the knife still was slashing through the air in such a way that it threatened at the very least to deprive the guard of his left ear and a goodly portion of his scalp besides.

As a result, the guard strode almost directly into the knife's path, still under the impression that Slater would not dare strike him with it. Neatly sidestepping the thrust of the Karl Gustav, Slater, as though doing a little jig on a dance floor, leapt up and, in coming down, sliced open the guard's tunic and much of his chest underneath. Then, like a mother embracing her son, he hugged the guard, clasping him with one hand while the other busied itself digging the knife in under his solar plexus and manipulating it around, cutting savagely into subcutaneous tissue and the vital organs that it protected. The guard flung aside his weapon and in an odd unexpected motion clutched hold of Slater as though to prop himself up against the pain.

Now the others concentrated all their attention on the struggling pair. This drama had taken an unexpected turn, and they were uncertain whether it pleased them. They still, of course, felt in control of the situation and could at any time—just as soon as the guard got out of their way—dispense of Slater with a single volley.

But Harry, recognizing that this was his opportunity, his sole chance, dived for the .44, flattening himself out against the floor and firing quickly at the two remaining guards. It was the force of the .44 cartridge he counted on, not the exact location it entered his targets. He hadn't the time to sight the gun, after all.

All his many years of practice had not been for naught. One bullet ascending up from the floor caught a guard in his kneecap. The injury was at once so painful and so debilitating that all the man could do in response was fire a fitful, ineffective blast of his gun toward the ceiling before flopping down against the far wall. The hardness of his landing caused his gun to fly away from him. Perhaps sensing that the odds had vastly altered, he made no effort to retrieve it. Instead he stayed where he was, trying futilely with his hands to staunch the flow of blood. Tears drained copiously from his eyes.

The second guard took a more serious injury as the .44 tore apart his intestines, sending up a great stench as feces oozed out of the wound. There was no possibility of retaliation from him. Surprise seemed to have frozen itself permanently on his face.

Slater, perhaps thinking that the situation had now been consolidated, allowed his eyes to wander and he stepped back from his dying victim, preparing to drop to the floor to escape the crossfire—should there be any crossfire.

Which may have explained why he failed to notice Virgilio who, having sought the relative sanctuary of the floor at the first report, now seized hold of the submachine gun that had fallen away from Slater's assailant. Virgilio had not emerged as a triumphant survivor from so many battles to die empty-handed; it would be a dishonor to exit from the earth, if that was his fate, without taking at least one of his enemies with him.

The Karl Gustav clattered in his hands. Splotches of blood appeared in sequence all down the length of Slater's body as though he were being spattered. But he was being completely riddled; that his body remained whole on the outside was a cruel deception, for on the inside there was nothing that was not pierced, shattered, or ruptured. Slater's eyes sought Harry's one last time and there was a sign of recognition in them, a sign of something else too, of friendship and forgiveness. Then he seemed all at once to diminish in size, to fade into something incorporeal, something that was just blood and air, no longer identifiable as an old mariner who had come to meet his death in this forbidden site in western Mexico.

Harry could not get a line of sight on Virgilio who had wisely taken shelter behind a giant, stone pre-Aztec god whose grotesque features seemed to mock the scene of death that was being played out before it. But neither could Virgilio seem able to find Harry in his sights, for Harry had taken refuge behind the couch where only ten minutes previously Virgilio had been probing the ample charms of his whore. Thick tufts of upholstery went flying into the air as the couch was perforated by successive rounds from the submachine gun, but Harry remained untouched.

Ignacio in the meantime was trying to crawl away, navigating himself between the four bodies that lay on the floor—only one of whom showed any sign of life at all: the guard with the demolished kneecap. Ignacio gasped and cried out for his madre whenever the fire from Virgilio's gun swept over his head. A journey to the Amazon would not have seemed as far to him as the one he was now attempting to make to the doorway.

Naturally, all this commotion was heard throughout the villa. Three men—another security detail—came running into the corridor that lay just beyond the threshold. They were sufficiently cautious not simply to rush the room, and so they contented themselves with digging in just beyond the exposed doorway.

But the only one who was doing any firing was Virgilio. Harry could have shot Ignacio, but he balked at putting a bullet into an unarmed man crawling to safety on his belly. And being unable to hit Virgilio, he decided to save what ammunition he had.

Virgilio kept on firing until he had expended his clip. But hearing only the groans of the surviving guard and the uproar in the corridor outside, he realized that he was accomplishing nothing by laying down a second barrage. He reloaded and called to Ignacio who had nearly attained his goal of the threshold.

"Tell them to rush the room!" he cried. This was spoken in Spanish, but Harry knew just enough of the language to catch the meaning. What Virgilio hoped was

157

that by drawing Harry's fire he could circle around and kill him himself. That others might be sacrificed so that he could execute his stratagem mattered nothing to him.

Ignacio crept out of the room, heaving a sigh of relief and offering up a prayer to several patron saints, and then proceeded to communicate Virgilio's directions to the security detail hunkered down in the corridor.

They obeyed without question. The first two, as soon as they were framed in the doorway, were brought down immediately. Harry held an excellent position, and his aim was as accurate as necessary. The reason he did not shoot the third was that the third, orders or no orders, had decided to withdraw.

Virgilio opened up again, infuriated that he had secured no additional advantage, but all he did was to gouge the couch out. He screamed at Harry, cursing him and himself for stupidly allowing this unhappy situation to develop. Then he screamed out to the corridor, upbraiding his men for failing to come to his aid. But they seemed determined not to meet the fate of those who already had complied with Virgilio's commands.

Though the situation threatened soon to become a stalemate, Harry understood the importance of making a hasty escape, not just from the Villa Corona but from the whole of Carangas and environs. But until his eyes again fell upon the pre-Aztec statue he could think of no way to accomplish this.

The statue, he now noticed, was not consistent in texture. Breaking the rough harsh stone surface that defined the statue was a small, narrow, smooth band that circled the neck. Harry deduced that this was where the statue had been repaired; it had been probably found in two pieces, head and torso. Previously, Harry had entertained no notions of penetrating the statue—it looked too sturdy, having already resisted what ravages time could visit on it. But there was an outside chance that if the .44 struck this ribbon of smoothness about the neck it could send the head tumbling down on Virgilio's more vulnerable one. Accordingly, Harry fired so that the trajectory of the bullet would impact directly against the rejoined neck. There was a loud walloping sound in response and a sudden spurt of dust and stone fragments. Then the hideous head rolled out of its mooring and dropped not on Virgilio's head but his foot. Virgilio let out a whoop of pain, hollering defiantly.

Without wasting a moment, Harry rushed forward, catching Virgilio unawares. Virgilio was too preoccupied in extricating his left foot from under the extraordinarily heavy head that lay on it to notice Harry until the .44 was pressed flush against his skull. Gazing up at his antagonist, he shook his head, still muttering with the pain, and said, "You are being most inconsiderate, señor. It is senseless for us both to die." He threw down the submachine gun, fully prepared to meet his maker, but this did not cause him to cease his efforts to get his foot free.

But on the contrary, Harry had no intention of hastening Virgilio's introduction to his maker (whichever maker would take the dubious honor of having been responsible for his creation). He viewed Virgilio as his passport out of this place. At last, with a pronounced groan, Virgilio succeeded in recovering his foot. He began to knead it with his hands, but Harry ordered him to stand. It was not easy, and the look he gave Harry was the look not of a heroin dealer or murderer but rather of an angry child.

"Must I stand up to be executed?"

"No execution now. We're taking a little trip."

Virgilio discerned Harry's plan and shrugged. He was not certain that this extension on his life made things better or worse. At the moment, however, he seemed to recognize the necessity of playing his role to the hilt. Four armed guards stood ready to clutter Harry's body up with 5.54mm cartridges. They certainly would have done so were it not for the fact that they would have to do the same to Virgilio's.

"Lower your weapons," Virgilio said, first in English for Harry's benefit, then in Spanish.

The guards appeared baffled by the request but did as they were instructed, allowing the two to pass.

Harry now was in possession of both the .44 and the Karl Gustav submachine gun, both of which discouraged anyone from attempting to rescue Virgilio, who grumpily dragged his injured foot behind him.

"Show me the laboratory," Harry said.

This directive obviously startled Virgilio. "You wish a guided tour—now?"

Harry was in no mood to discuss his motives. Spying Ignacio who slunk against the wall, curiously eyeing the two, he called out to him. Whatever he said was incomprehensible to Harry, but somehow Harry caught the sense of it simply by the intonation. He abruptly whipped around, spinning Virgilio with him. Ignacio was now armed and had with some difficulty produced a handgun of some kind from his pocket. Harry allowed him no opportunity and fired simultaneously with both the .44 and the submachine gun.

Ignacio crashed back against the wall, aghast that he had lost this one opportunity to demonstrate that he was no coward, then slowly drifted to the floor. His glasses slipped off and in his final moments of life it was his glasses that he groped for. He wanted one last clear look of the world before he departed it. He never got it.

Virgilio looked from the lifeless form of his partner to Harry and gave him one of his customary shrugs. Life was hard, it was over easily, he would have said had he been inclined to say anything at all.

Two of the tunic-gowned figures appeared and stooped down by Ignacio to see if medical assistance might help him. Determining that it would not, they turned him over so that they wouldn't have to look at him any longer.

The sentry at the door leading down to the laboratory, where the heroin was derived from the morphine base, was unwilling to admit Harry even with Virgilio. He evidently thought that he could reason with Harry for he addressed him in a Spanish so rapid he couldn't get one word out without a second overtaking it. Harry, having neither the time nor patience to listen to his gibbering, simply knocked him aside with the Karl Gustav. Virgilio gave Harry one of his suspect smiles.

"You can be most persuasive when you want."

Strangely, Virgilio showed no trace of nervousness, not in his manner nor in his voice. His sense of fatalism allowed him a kind of freedom.

Peering down a short flight of stairs Harry could see only a welter of burners, pipes, sinks, and trays filled with what looked like chemical solutions. Men in white, not all of them Mexican, were toiling over their chemicals, carrying out their tasks in an antiseptic atmosphere that vaguely reminded Harry of an operating theater. The smell reminded him of something as well, but he could not say just what it was. But it was heavy in the air, almost sickening.

To Virgilio he said, "Tell all of them to leave."

So absorbed were most of these people that they took scant notice of Harry and their employer standing at the head of the stairs. Virgilio's voice surprised them. They raised their eyes to him in confusion. Then Harry began shooting at all the equipment, shattering glass and demolishing some of the elaborate machinery that had been set up for the distillation process. This reinforced the impact of Virgilio's words, and the air was filled with plaintive screams and cries of alarm as the chemists and their assistants scrambled for the exits.

Harry's bullets hit something that was obviously combustible because suddenly flames shot up from perhaps three or four different locations in the laboratory; with the enveloping smoke it was difficult to determine exactly.

"We only will rebuild this, you know," Virgilio said, almost chiding him. Still, he admitted that it would be a rather costly loss. The smoke from the fire began to waft up in their direction. Harry supposed that he had done enough, maybe more than enough, for Keepnews. Now his only objective was to save his ass. For that he was going to have to rely on Virgilio once again.

But the fact was that with the fire spreading so rapidly, consuming the Villa Corona with ease, no one seemed to be paying attention to Harry or Virgilio any longer. It looked like every man for himself. All the inhabitants of the compound were fleeing in the direction of the lush tropical vegetation, which was already alive with the vicious chatter of birds adding to the human cries of alarm.

The Land Rover was where Ignacio had left it. But it was obviously too much of a temptation, for already five men were attempting to clamber into it. Harry, still keeping the .44 pressed to Virgilio's back, advanced unhurriedly toward the vehicle. He raised the Karl Gustav so that it was targeted directly on the man who had just taken the wheel. The man, sputtering from the smoke that had infiltrated his lungs, looked vastly surprised to find somebody impeding his way. His four passengers, greedy for prompt movement, were not especially pleased to see him either.

Thinking that the problem Harry presented to them would be easily enough solved by running him over, the driver gunned the jeep forward. Virgilio, mindless of the threat of the .44, leapt out of the way but Harry held his position and fired a round. The driver's forehead turned bright scarlet and he lurched back over the seat. The Land Rover swerved off to the side, coming to a rest against the side of a palm that buckled but finally did not give way. Seeing their driver killed like this inspired the four others to choose another means of escape. They had no stomach for fighting while the fire raced across the brush that sprouted immediately outside the villa. Flames spewed from the windows. The air, torrid enough to begin with, grew hotter still as the blaze whipped up and through the tiled roof. Harry was astonished that the structure could go up so fast. It was in its own way a rather impressive sight.

By pushing the dead driver out of the way Harry was able to get himself behind the wheel. The jeep had not been critically damaged in its collision with the palm. The tires spun as the jeep regained a more accommodating surface.

Virgilio was screaming to two armed men to stop Harry. But the two men were much too interested in escaping the fire to listen to Virgilio. This so infuriated him that he attempted to stop one of them forcibly, upbraiding him for his cowardice.

The man might or might not have recognized that this was his employer. But it was plain to see that he did not wish to have anyone distract him at a time such as this. He attempted to push on. Virgilio wouldn't let him. He began to tug on the man's revolver; if no one else was going to do so, he would kill Harry himself.

But Virgilio had evidently chosen the wrong individual to harass. The man balked at surrendering his gun and instead uncocked it. Virgilio didn't appear to notice. The man then squeezed the trigger. Virgilio was so close to him that the shot was muffled. A large ring-like gunpowder stain formed on his shirtfront. Virgilio released his grip and tottered backward. For good measure, the man shot him again. This time he did notice. He did a steady march backward, clutching his stomach. He kept taking his hands away to stare at the blood that was accumulating in them. Then he would shake his head as if in disbelief and continue his uncertain progress to the rear. At last he came to a halt, and a very thoughtful, if somewhat dazed, expression crossed his face. This was not how he had expected it to end. He decided that all things considered he would sit down. He remained sitting for several minutes, wondering why he was not dead yet. Blood flowed so plentifully from the two wounds that it created a large puddle between his legs, so large that every so often he'd shift position so he wouldn't become too wet.

He stayed where he was, his dying a protracted affair, until the fire caught up with him, tracing its path across the thick verdancy of the terrain. And when the fire did reach him, he made only the slightest effort to move. Then he realized it wasn't worth it. He thought it most unfortunate that Harry had survived and he had not. It would not have even been too bad if they had both been killed. Possibly, he reflected, someone else would do his work for him.

Chapter Sixteen

"They're not coming," Vincent said, staring over the gunwales. Carangas was fading gradually into the thickening dusk, receding into the darkness of the shoreline. Bursts of feeble light were all that separated the town from the surrounding forests.

"What makes you think so?" Max asked casually, running a cloth over the carbine he held in his hands. He hadn't let go of the gun since Booth and Vincent had returned to the boat. Booth and Vincent had agreed that they would kill Max, throw him overboard, and set off on their way. After all, hadn't Garcia assured them that there would be no problem with Harry and Slater, that they would be disposed of?

But Max's intrusive presence and his determination to keep hold of his weapon at all times made killing him a more formidable proposition than they had imagined.

"Sooner or later the fucker has to go to sleep," Vincent said, and Booth, despite his impatience, had agreed. Why risk a fight, whose outcome could not be guaranteed, when a knife across the jugular while Max lay dreaming was so much more efficient?

But though this plan had its merits neither of the two men could have foreseen that Max would be so determined to remain here, moored in the harbor of Carangas, until Harry and the skipper came back. Nor could they afford to divulge to Max the information they had acquired from Garcia, not without arousing his suspicion.

"We'll wait until tomorrow. Then if they don't come

we'll go into Carangas and see what happened to them," announced Max. He was clearly not putting his suggestion up for a vote.

Booth and Vincent observed him with disgust, and yet they did not complain. Sometime, they believed, between now and then he would fall asleep, and then they could get on with the journey.

The darkness was nearly total when Max suddenly ascended to the top of the pilothouse and looked out to the sea. The two mates had long since given up scrutinizing the waters or even paying heed to Max's movements. Sooner or later he would give up his vigil; that was the only moment they were waiting for.

Max wisely said nothing about the object he discerned approaching the *Confrontation*. Instead he watched it as it came nearer. Little by little it revealed itself as a small skiff, hardly seaworthy. Who was in it he could not see. Then he realized there was just one man, straining against the current to maneuver the craft in toward the yacht.

It was only when Harry was climbing up the rope ladder to the deck that Booth realized that everything had changed. He went down below to alert Vincent. "This wasn't supposed to fucking happen," he said.

Being of a slightly more philosophic bent, Vincent couldn't see that there was any point worrying about it. At least there was no sign of Slater; that meant one less person to contend with. "We'll just have to be patient," Vincent counseled.

"And what if they discover the shit?"

Vincent dismissed Booth's concern with a flick of his hand.

"We hid it away too perfectly. They're not going to find it. The problem is with you Booth, you worry too fucking much. You get ulcers that way."

"Fuck you! Ulcers, my ass."

In spite of his outburst, he made no serious objection to what Vincent had said. He was just sorely disappointed to have encountered such ill-fortune so early in the game.

165

Up on deck Harry and Max took the helm, alternating on an hourly basis. Given the way events had transpired in Carangas and at the nearby Villa Corona it would not have been wise to linger about the harbor.

Because of this unlikely turn of events, and deprived of Slater's companionship, Harry found that he had no one to talk to except Max. This discovery, which he had given no thought to until he'd safely reached the boat, was a confounding one for Harry. Never having regarded Max as someone to even say good morning to, let alone befriend, he found that it was either Max or nothing. To his great surprise, he realized that it could have been worse— it could have been just Booth and Vincent.

"They wanted to leave you two behind," Max said, very suddenly, apropos of nothing. Two and a half hours had passed since they had left Carangas behind.

"What did you say?"

Max repeated his words, then proceeded to clarify them. "They were sure you and Slater would not be coming back. They seemed convinced like someone had told them so."

"They didn't elaborate?"

"To me? Are you kidding? The only reason they didn't go anywhere is because they knew I might have blown them both away." He gestured to the carbine that rested on the seat below the VHF receiver.

"I see," Harry said though the fact was he didn't quite see. Was it conceivable that the two had somehow been in on the scheme to entrap and kill them?

"I liked Slater. Poor dumb guy. But I really liked him." Max looked to Harry for some form of corroboration.

"I liked him too, Max," he said, clapping him on the shoulder.

"Where are you going, Harry?"

"Below deck. You stay at the wheel, make sure you keep north by northwest."

"Will do. And Harry, you be careful of those bastards."

166

Harry didn't give him an answer, but he smiled. That was all the answer Max needed anyhow.

Below deck everything appeared to be normal. The only sound was the monotonous stirring of the water against the hull, nothing else. From the aft staterooms, where Booth and Vincent slept, there was nothing to be heard. No light was visible beneath their doors. Harry presumed that they were either asleep or, for some reason, pretending to be.

Having no idea why he was down here, what clue he could possibly find that would enlighten him to the mates' motives, he returned to the pilothouse. Something, he felt, was very wrong, but he could not determine what it was. While he held utter contempt for the two men he could not allow his personal feelings to intrude. But on the other hand, the last thing he wanted to do was doze off while they were awake. They did not inspire confidence in seeing the sun again.

"Max, did you see anything unusual when Vincent and Booth got back?"

Max tried to think. When he did this a strange glint came into his eyes. "No, not really. They got back this afternoon, oh, I'd say about three. But nothing unusual, no."

Harry shrugged. "It's not important . . ."

The glint in his eyes grew more luminous. "Wait a minute! I did notice something. Right after they got back they went to work fixing leaks. Well, just maybe two leaks. You know that shit we've got on board? Epoxy shit, works OK, Glu-it I think it's called. I was watching them, they didn't see me. But I figured it was weird, them fixing leaks all of a sudden. I didn't know we had any in particular. Slater mentioned nothing to me about any leaks."

"Max, you think you could point out those leaks they were closing up?"

Max thought he could. He led Harry into the galley and hoisting the rug, indicated a glazed patch of teakwood. "This is one. The other is in the utility closet."

He was prepared to stand there in the half-light of the galley and watch Harry perform the excavation, but Harry had no desire to have him hanging about. To say that he trusted Max more than Booth and Vincent was not to imply that he trusted him completely. "You mind going back up to the deck? I don't like the idea of running on automatic for too long."

"Why? There's nothing out there but water." But Max complied, a bit offended that he could not lend further assistance to Harry.

As soon as the sound of his footsteps up the stairway faded, Harry set to work, using the instruments he found handy in the galley: steak knife, opener, corkscrew, fork. He continued chopping and scooping, little by little enlarging the hole in the floor. He was so absorbed by this task that he lost track of time. Minutes might have passed or the better part of an hour, he had no idea. But at last he had succeeded in exposing a hollow that just that afternoon had been created. It was not large, but then it didn't have to be. The glassine bags he brought into view fitted perfectly inside it. Though he already knew what the bags contained, Harry tore open one of them, poked a finger in among the granules, and tasted what he came up with. Heroin. And a very fine grade of it at that.

"Find what you're looking for?"

The voice caught him by surprise. He swiveled about, still kneeling, and saw Booth looming over him. Vincent was nowhere in sight. Harry deduced that he must have gone up for Max.

In Booth's hands was the AKS that had once been the possession of Francis before Max's knife had cut short his life. As much as he might have preferred the intimacy of a knife, Booth was respectful enough of Harry's facility with a gun to employ one himself.

Harry looked from Booth to the heroin and back again. "Yes, I think I did," he said.

Max was bored. He had never been one to appreciate the beauties of nature and neither the greatness of the

168

ocean nor the profusion of stars overhead held any interest for him. The control panel before him showed that everything was as it should be, that there were no shoals to be concerned with, no other craft that might get in the *Confrontation*'s way any time soon. The maritime channels and the international weather reports were similarly without fascination for him. He located some AM station on the portable radio, which was broadcasting out of San Diego. Periodically the station would fade, yielding to static, and Max would have to tune it back again. But the rock music emerging from the radio was not so loud that it drowned out the fall of a man's feet against the deck.

At first, Max assumed that it was Harry, and he turned eagerly to ask him just what he had found concealed under the teakwood floor. But he saw now that it wasn't Harry at all, it was Vincent, and that he was armed with one of the Mark 9s.

Max wasn't rational enough to judge his chances or contemplate his risks. With the first sign of danger all thought process in his mind was blotted out. Because he never truly considered the possibility he might die—he'd survived every previous engagement he'd been in, against the laws of probability—he simply grabbed hold of his Mark 9 and fired—just as Vincent did.

Hearing the shots, Booth raised his eyes, sufficiently distracted by the commotion that his attention was no longer solely on Harry.

When he fixed his eyes on him again he was horrified by what he saw. Harry did not have a weapon in his hand—he'd had no chance to extricate his Magnum or to get to the .22 strapped to his ankle. But he had had the opportunity to draw his lighter out of his pocket and now a high yellow-blue flame danced from it. The heroin glimmered in the light it produced. Looking Booth evenly in the eyes, Harry said matter-of-factly, "No way you're going to kill me before this goes up in flames."

Fire seemed somehow to be an ally of Harry this day.

Booth recalled Garcia's warning. To bring in only

169

half the heroin—the half hidden in the floor of the utility closet—was to implicate him and Vincent in the theft of the other half. How many thousands of dollars would be lost was something Booth did not know. What he did know was that his life—he couldn't care less about Vincent's—was utterly worthless if Harry made good on his threat.

Booth did not have any idea now what he should do. He could not bring himself to remove his eyes from the tiny flame burning so very close to the heroin. The frustration he was suffering was so immense that he was tempted to shoot Harry just to make it go way. Still, he had enough sense to realize that this option had just been foreclosed to him, at least temporarily. "Well, then you and me, we'll just wait and see," he said. He meant this as a threat, but it didn't come across that way.

Harry realized he wanted to consult with Vincent before taking any definitive action. He had heard no more shots after the first two. But whether that meant Vincent had triumphed or Max, or neither, he could not begin to imagine.

Vincent was still in shock, but he was functioning. Every so often he would glance down at his arm, what was left of it anyhow. Max's bullet had passed clean through it, right above the elbow, shattering the bone so that a fragment of it now protruded from the bloody flesh.

The carbine he'd been holding had been forced from his hand and lay at his feet. But each time he attempted to retrieve it the pain got the better of him—the old pain this was, the pain from Francis' machete.

Max had not escaped unscathed. Blood was soaking his trousers, erupting from the wound in his groin. But he did not appear to notice. Instead he moved, slowly, but methodically, across the deck, a marine knife clutched in his hand.

Vincent thought of running but for several moments did nothing, immobilized by the pain and yet still convinced he could, in spite of it, get ahold of the carbine and kill Max before he came any closer.

Max was daring him to do just that. "I'm giving you a chance, sucker," he said. But there really wasn't any great acrimony in his words—he was the matador moving in for the kill. The wound in his groin made no difference. He was happy in his anticipation and absolutely oblivious of Harry's plight. He had in fact altogether forgotten about Harry in the excitement of the moment.

Desperate, recognizing that he had this one chance and only this one, Vincent threw himself on the deck and fastened his one good hand on the Mark 9. But before he could do anything with it, Max leaped on him and with several quick decisive slices of his knife, perforated Vincent all up and down his back. He was so determined, he put so much sheer force into the stabbing that occasionally he would stick the blade all the way through Vincent and into the deck, thereby impaling him. Vincent screamed, but because his mouth was so close to the deck, no sound emerged outside of a muffled gasp. Blood shot up through the several wounds Max had made, spattering him so much that it looked as though he'd been completely dunked in it. At last Vincent ceased squirming in a futile effort to free himself. It took several moments longer before Max realized that he was as dead as he was ever going to be.

Almost reluctantly, he drew himself off his victim. Now the pain in his groin asserted itself. He was about to do something to staunch the bleeding when he remembered Harry. And by remembering Harry he remembered Booth.

Though he was clumsy by nature and not inclined to use stealth when he could just blunder into a situation, he had enough wits about him not to simply rush down the stairs. This, he realized, could invite a quick and painful death.

And it also occurred to him that no one below deck would know who was still alive, Vincent or him. He opened the hatch, extinguished the overhead light, then fired Vincent's Mark 9 down into the cabin. He knew his shots would not hit anybody—he wasn't aiming at any target—but they might very well bring someone into the open.

As soon as the light was doused, Booth's expression took on a frenzied cast. He did not know what was happening. "Vincent? Vincent? Is that you, Vincent?"

All he received by way of response was a sudden staccato of rifle fire. It caused him to tremble, to shift to the left, still training his AKS on Harry, who complacently remained where he was, holding his lighter over the heroin and hoping that he would not run out of fluid any time soon.

"Vincent? Vincent? What was that shit?"

Another fusillade sounded. Glass popped and something else gave way and crashed to the floor.

"Cocksucker! You stay put, you stay put!" Booth stammered. This was all really too much for him; his mind was not equipped to handle situations that got this complicated.

"I have no intention of going anywhere," Harry told him.

The calmness of his voice further infuriated Booth. His face had gone white, sweat moistened his skin.

"Vincent?" he called again. The panic was audible in his voice.

"Coming!"

Booth visibly relaxed. Though Harry recognized the voice as Max's Booth had not. He had wanted to hear Vincent, he was desperate to hear Vincent, and so he had.

"I got the fucker here, Vincent, I got him here."

He was smiling at Harry, assured now that this whole enterprise was going to be successful.

So it was that Booth did not turn around when the footsteps sounded on the stairs behind him. "You going to take him out or should I do the honors?" Booth asked, momentarily forgetful that until the threat to their ship-

172

ment was disposed of no one was going to take out Harry.

"You do it," Max said, making no effort to disguise his voice.

The look on Booth's face was a wonder to behold. His eyes bugged out, his face returned to its previous ashen state. Whatever words he had ready caught in his throat. He spun around, but not nearly so quickly as he should have.

Harry didn't wait. He had his Magnum out and shot it just as Max's knife flew into Booth's throat. Almost simultaneously, as he staggered backward toward Harry the .44 flung him in the reverse direction. Enough life remained in him to pull the trigger on his AKS and hold it tight, but he did nothing more than ravage the ceiling of the cabin. Then, abandoning his weapon, he brought both hands up to his neck, though in his last seconds of life he retracted his left hand so he could get a good sense of what the .44's exit wound was like. It was very big and fatal.

Max regarded Harry, distracted from the injury in his groin which was now filling his sneakers up with so much blood that they were dyed red.

"How's that for team effort?" he declared proudly.

Harry took one look at the bloodied figure in front of him and shrugged. "Vincent?"

"Feeling no pain."

Harry understood. He drew the lighter closer to the heroin, close enough for it to ignite.

"What's that?" Max asked, but with only minimal curiosity.

"Are you hurt?" Max was coated with so much blood by now that it looked almost as if he'd been turned inside out.

Max appeared to think about this for some time. "I think I am. I think that bastard Vincent shot me. It sure hurts like hell."

"Well, why don't you get washed up and I'll take a look at it?"

The heroin made a strange, faintly crackling sound as

the fire took to it. It was a more satisfying means of disposing of it than simply tossing it into the sea.

Chapter Seventeen

On the edge of Golden Gate Park, about twenty feet above the coastal highway, overlooking the Cliff House restaurant and extending for some distance beyond it, are a series of artificial rock formations, simulated caves. From the outside there would be no way of determining that the massive boulder-like rocks are not genuinely a part of the landscape. In fact they are hollowed out. To reach these caves it is necessary to go around in back and penetrate by means of narrow passageways that are known mostly to teenagers who have left as their legacy empty beer cans, used condoms, and the occasional depleted bottle of Wild Turkey.

The purpose of these phony caves is easily enough discerned. For there on the dirt floor, among the pebbles and human detritus, is a swivel block upon which a gun emplacement was once supposed to be mounted. The first detonation of the gun presumably would eliminate the false barrier over the highway, yielding a spectacular view of the Pacific. These caves were constructed during World War II in the eventuality that the Japanese launched a seaborne invasion. The Japanese never did, and the guns were never installed. Aside from nocturnal visits by lusting teenagers the caves remained empty.

Until now.

Nicholas Cimentini looked well and rested. Whatever stress he'd been under since his arrest had not adversely affected him. On this particular day, shortly after noon, he sat at a table strategically positioned to allow him and his two companions, Trime and Esser, an unrivaled view of the Seal Rocks and the sparkling blue waters of the

174

Pacific Ocean. The bay was well populated on this late summer day, dotted with the billowing masts of nearly two dozen sailboats that listed precariously in the wakes stirred up by the powerboats and ferries.

The meal that Nicholas—Father Nick—had set before him was one of the Cliff House's specialties: sautéed king crab meat topped with a brandied cream sauce. "I know," Father Nick laughed, observing the dour expressions of his dining companions, "I know what the doctors told me. I swore off this kind of stuff. But you got to give a guy a break. Even priests suffer relapses." His eyes were drawn back to the coastal waters far below. "And besides, this is a rather special day. I feel like celebrating."

Trime and Esser, both austere-looking gentlemen who had been responsible for laundering Father Nick's vast inflow of cash for several years, had no idea what he was talking about. Nor were they certain they much cared for his animated manner. Father Nick was not usually so genial, so outgoing. When he got this way, it was cause for alarm.

Trime and Esser were both thin men. They ate because that was the only way they were ever going to survive. But unlike Father Nick, they seldom displayed a genuine interest in what sort of food they were consuming. And being of practical natures, they preferred holding business discussions in an atmosphere free of spider plants, stuffed couches, brass railings, and spectacular views of the Pacific Ocean; a windowless room with dull beige walls they felt was far more conducive to getting to the matter at hand.

They were here, so far as they knew, for the purpose of considering just how they would invest all the proceeds from the burgeoning Mexican operation. The way they spoke, it might as well have been the sugar market or the interest rates on that week's treasury notes they were discussing, not the transport and sale of pure-grade heroin.

The problem they were encountering, however, was that Father Nick seemed incapable of concentrating. Here they had it all down on paper, figures upon figures, vast sums added and subtracted and subdivided, and all he kept doing was looking out the damn window and savoring every bite of his king crab. Trime and Esser had outlined a whole catalogue of front operations that were worth putting money in—laundromats and pizza parlors, Reno casinos and Manhattan hotels, massage parlors and tax-shelter movie deals. But each time they thought they had made a point, all they would get in response was a blank look. Father Nick was known for his quick grasp of facts, his formidable powers of memory, but today he seemed capable of grasping nothing whatsoever.

"What was that you said, Tom?" he addressed Esser. Then he laughed as though it were all a great joke, the point of which neither of his guests could guess.

By dessert and coffee, when they should have begun grappling with the details, gotten down to brass tacks, as it were, Father Nick had ceased paying attention to them entirely. Now he was beginning more and more to glance at his watch, a digital device that kept popping red phosphorescent numbers out of an empty black field.

Then he turned away from Esser and Trime so that he could scrutinize the bay. Though his physicians had warned him to stay away from alcohol as well as from dishes heavy in chloresterol, he was ignoring their advice. His fifth—or was it his sixth?—martini rested in his hand. One pack of cigarettes lay exhausted on the table, and he'd begun a second. Still, these were the only outward signs of increasing nervousness. Otherwise he retained his apparent good humor. The successive drinks had made him just slightly more taciturn, less inclined to play host, but that was all the impact they seemed to have had.

Suddenly Father Nick's face lit up; for on this warm September afternoon it had become Christmas just as it should have for a man whose nickname enjoyed such widespread recognition.

There, just visible on the bay, steering a steady course between a Hatteras and a thirty-foot masthead ketch, was Harold Keepnews' yacht *Confrontation*. Father Nick had never actually seen it before, but he had studied photographs enough to recognize it. The photographs had been shot from virtually all possible angles in the harbor of Carangas and flown up to San Francisco three days previously.

"Half an hour late," Father Nick muttered. Esser and Trime looked at him bewilderedly, having no idea what he was referring to. "But I'll forgive them." He then turned back to his guests; it was almost as though he were surprised to see the two of them still there. "You will excuse me, gentlemen, I have to make a phone call. I will be right back."

Way below Point Lobos Avenue, where Cliff House was situated (1090 to be exact), hidden in among the outcroppings that defined the steep descent of the land into the sea, was a solitary man who held two objects in his hands—one was a thermos filled with cold water to relieve him from the hot afternoon sun, the other was a CB radio. It was the second object upon which he focused his concentration now.

"Have you subject in range, Delta-five?"

The man now raised the binoculars strapped over his chest to his eyes and studied the horizon. A few moments passed, and then the prow of the yacht came within sight.

"Confirm, Sigma. Subject in range."

"Ten-four."

To the diners in the Cliff House it sounded like a thunderclap, but a glimpse of the sky revealed no sign that this could possibly be; not a cloud was visible in the blue expanse.

From the mountain above, rock and cement, ground into pulverized fragments, came tumbling down, strewing the coast highway with a large heap of rubble that caused traffic going both directions to halt.

Higher still, what had once looked like the sheer stone surface of a boulder had almost completely disintegrated, revealing in its place a big black hole, from which a Soviet-constructed .82mm howitzer protruded. There was a second explosion, a thick cloud of smoke, and a sudden tongue of fire in its midst.

Out of the bay, scarcely a moment later, water shot up like a geyser, and the boats in its vicinity rocked violently in response.

"Sigma, this is Delta-five. I would say five degrees up."

"We read you, Delta-five. Five degrees up. Ten-four."

A second blast produced the same concussive sound and eruption of smoke and fire. But in this instance the angle of the gun had been adjusted correctly.

Harry, having radioed ahead to Keepnews to tell him to expect his boat back, adding that they were three crewmen short (without elaborating), had not known exactly what kind of welcome he would get—if any. But whatever he'd imagined it had not been anything like this.

As soon as the first shell plummeted down directly ahead of the *Confrontation* and slightly off to the port-side, heaving up water so that the yacht careened dangerously on the crest of each succeeding wave, Harry had understood all too well that his vessel was the target. But still he was slow to react if only because this was possibly the last thing that he had expected—to be plunged into such an unequal military engagement.

Worse was the fact that he had to operate the boat by himself. Though Max had been quick to dismiss the groin wound he'd sustained as insignificant and though Harry had sought to minister to it, relying on what practical medical experience he'd picked up over the years, the bullet had penetrated too far into the muscle to be easily excised. And while Harry had provided him with whatever antibiotics were available to them, an infection had sprung up the night following their flight from Carangas. Max had refused special attention, insisting that they would arrive in San Francisco soon enough without him being airlifted off the boat. And besides, as he had reminded Harry, Keepnews was not likely to put out any money to rescue him, considering who he was and what his relationship to Wendy had been.

But just that morning Max's fever had grown worse, and he now lay listless on his bed, suffering in silence, suffering all the more with the yacht's crazy keeling motion.

Harry struggled to maintain the wheel and keep the yacht from running aground. But his struggle was futile. With the waters in such tumult from the first bombardment there was no way he was going to gain mastery over the craft. And then, twenty seconds later, the second shell was lobbed into the bay, this one at a much more accurate trajectory. Harry could see the mountainside belch out fire and smoke and knew what to expect. Not that that did any good.

The shell caught the *Confrontation* amidships, blasting a hole all the way down into the cabin and out the hull. The yacht broke into two, each half capsizing in a different direction. Was it always going to be his lot to drown in San Francisco Bay, Harry wondered, as he was thrown back and forth against the sides of the pilothouse, which was now so sharply angled that it was just a couple of feet from meeting the ocean full on.

Harry could not decide whether he was hurt or hurt so badly that he could not count on his body. The old pain in his leg was reawakened, he knew that much, but he could still work it. Blood was slipping down from his scalp, but the injury did not seem substantial. It was difficult to determine the situation with any precision, especially when he was being hurled this way and that while seawater assaulted him on all sides.

Max! He suddenly remembered that Max was down in the master stateroom. He could not allow him to drown. After all, he'd promised Wendy he'd save the bastard's ass and he meant to do so—particularly since he truly felt an obligation to Max, Wendy or no Wendy.

There was no further shelling. The mountain above the coast highway went silent, and gradually the water surrounding the *Confrontation* grew more tranquil.

Nothing remained to be seen of the stern-half of the yacht; of the bow-half only the pilothouse remained partially above water.

There were other boats visible, but they had, wisely, withdrawn as fast as possible, their captains fearing that they too would be shelled if they lingered too long in the neighborhood.

So it would be a while before Harry could expect any help. With no other option left to him, he swam, not certain where exactly he was destined but hoping that he had the general direction down right. Underwater, the yacht's configuration was a shadowy, spectral thing; nothing seemed substantial. He located a hatch and tugged hard until he forced it open.

There, gripping the teakwood supports upon which the hatch rested, was Max. Blood had welled up in such profusion that at first it was almost impossible to see him.

Harry seized hold of him, dragging him up toward the surface, his only thought to get some air into his lungs before the pain overwhelmed him. At last he broke through, his arms locked about Max's jaw. As he continued laboriously to swim toward shore, a trail of blood spread in the water behind him. All of it, or most of it anyhow, was coming from Max. "You're going to live, goddamnit," Harry muttered to him, though it was doubtful Max could hear. "I'm not doing all this for nothing." He was angry, raging, and it was the anger, more than anything else, that propelled him onward.

Struggling against the currents, in water that was—despite the atmospheric temperature—unusually cold, Harry managed finally to attain a small beachhead that was completely empty: a forlorn stretch of sand in the shadow of jutting rocks. He pulled Max onto the dry surface and for the first time looked closely at his face. His eyes were open, so was his mouth, but the eyes were vacant and the mouth engorged with seawater.

Then Harry allowed his eyes to continue their inspection; where, he wondered, was the source of all this blood? He did not need to search too far for an answer.

The blood was still pulsing out but at a diminished rate. One did not require an extensive medical background to see why this was so. The truth of the matter was that there was very little blood left to drain out of Max; for directly below his knee, in a terrible even line, something big and sharp, dislodged by the blast, had sheared off his extremities. Max had been dead, or nearly so, when Harry had found him. His rescue effort had been in vain.

Chapter Eighteen

Harold Keepnews was a shattered man. When Harry appeared before him he was scarcely able to recognize him. He sat in the living room, with the curtains drawn against the intrusion of light, a drink in his trembling hand and Rossini playing on the turntable. He seemed to have aged prematurely. His eyes hinted at a protracted period of insomnia compounded by heavy drinking, perhaps pills. There were no servants about, no gardener. And above all, no wife.

When Harry sat down beside him and briefed him on what had happened, sparing nothing in his account of the Mexican adventure and the fiasco upon his return, Keepnews scarcely seemed interested. That he had lost his skipper and a second yacht that had cost him nearly a quarter of a million dollars apparently made little difference to him.

"I am glad that you got out alive," Keepnews said, though the fact was he didn't appear to be glad about anything whatsoever. "I saw in the papers that all were thought lost."

That was fine with Harry. The fewer questions he had to answer the better. As far as he knew, no one had been aware he was on the yacht in the first place. No one except for the men who wished to see him dead.

Harry did his best to cast a favorable light on the operation even so, emphasizing the destruction of the heroin lab in the Villa Corona, but he did this mostly to buoy Keepnews's spirits. He realized that whatever damage he had inflicted on the operation managed by the late Señors Virgilio and Ignacio Mendoza, it would only be a temporary irritant to the drug dealers, not a major setback. There were too many Ignacios and Virgilios in the world ready to replace the ones who lay moldering in the jungle.

Harold did not seem to be listening to him. "You tried," he said, practically inaudibly, "I suppose that's what counts." He did not sound the least bit convinced. Then, abruptly, he threw his head back, and tears sprang to his eyes. "She's gone!" he cried out in such pain that Harry winced and turned away. "She's gone," he repeated. "For good."

"Wendy?" It was the first time he dared mention her name.

"Wendy, yes." He rubbed his eyes with a handkerchief, suddenly embarrassed at this uncustomary display of emotion. He breathed hard in an effort to compose himself. "What is maddening, what is absolutely infuriating, is that we had just had a reconciliation. Only a week ago. Less than a week actually—six days. She'd moved out, but then, Sunday night, she called me and said she wanted to see if we could make a go of it again." He was talking as though he were in a trance—his recitation had a practiced, lifeless ring to it.

Six days ago, Harry reckoned, he was on his way out of Carangas. He wondered at how close and how far away Carangas and Sunday were to him.

"And then?" Harry prodded him.

"And then when I woke up Thursday morning I found her gone. All her belongings, what she hadn't taken before, all were gone. There was no note, nothing. It would appear she doesn't even want the house anymore."

It was on Thursday that the *Confrontation* had been attacked. Harry had gone underground for a day, hoping to recuperate sufficiently so that he could finally face Keepnews. He began to think that possibly Wendy's timing and the fate of the *Confrontation* might be somehow linked, but he decided to say nothing.

"Harry, I don't believe there's any chance of seeing her again. I am enough of a realist to know that. But with her gone, I no longer have any ambition. I sit here, I have been sitting here since she left, except for going to the bathroom. I have sent all the staff away. Their presence was a humiliation for me. I never realized that one person could exert such a hold over another. Does this sound melodramatic to you? It must, coming from me." He let out a bitter laugh. "But I swear to you it is the truth. I would never have believed that she would leave me finally. That she would take on other lovers, like that Max—" He spat out the name in contempt. "Well, I could tolerate that. I didn't like it but I could tolerate it so long as she stayed with me, came back to me in the end. But this!" He shook his head in bewilderment.

"Tell me," Harry put in gently, "have you any idea where she went?"

Slowly, almost grudgingly, Keepnews answered. "Yes, yes, I have an idea. I am not without resources. She is right now in Sausalito. I have the address."

"A house she rented? Friends she moved in with?"

"Not friends. Friend, singular."

"A man?"

"A man I think you know. A man who Wendy knew represented all I despised, all I have spent my life fighting against. She chose him deliberately. He has a rather high-spirited life-style. It was not difficult for her to arrange an 'accidental' encounter. Wendy seldom exhibits any ambition. Only when something, or rather someone, interests her enough will she bring her full talents to bear on the situation. Generally she gets who and what she wants."

Thinking of her ardent pursuit of him, Harry could do nothing but agree with her demoralized husband.

"And the name of the man?" Harry had a feeling he already knew but wanted the confirmation.

"The name of the man is Nicholas Cimentini."

Harry spent all of Saturday afternoon, following his interview with Keepnews, wandering through downtown Sausalito, surveying the docks where yachts less endangered than the *Confrontation* and the *Hyacinth* were coming into berth, lingering in the restaurants and cafes on Main Street, strolling into the boutiques, galleries, and antique stores where he thought it likely Wendy might come, but there was no sign of her or of Father Nick. Presumably, they remained secluded in Father Nick's house nestled farther up on the wooded hillside.

It seemed clear to Harry, as clear as things ever got anyway, that Wendy had stage-managed the reconciliation at Father Nick's behest so that she could ascertain what was happening to the *Confrontation* in its journey back to the States. How she had obtained her information, by spying on her husband or simply turning an attentive ear to him when he confided the facts in the warmth of post-coital affection, was of secondary importance. The point was it wouldn't have been difficult for her to learn what she wanted. It was possible, even likely, that she'd been the one responsible for betraying them in Carangas. She always seemed to know every detail of her husband's business—there was no reason she wouldn't have learned of Harry's radio transmission. Just the fact that he had survived was evidence enough that the plot conceived in Carangas had failed to materialize. By mentioning that three crewmen had been lost, Harry had unwittingly provided further confirmation that Booth and Vincent were dead and that the heroin they were taking back with them was destroyed. That was sufficient information to set Father Nick's plan in motion to blow the *Confrontation*—and with it Harry and Max—out of the water.

It was Wendy's motives that Harry could not quite fathom. Was her hatred of her husband so pronounced that she was willing to go to such lengths simply to humiliate and finally destroy him? Was she seeking revenge against Harry, in addition, because she felt he had run out on her? Did she harbor some unarticulated grievance against Max as well that could only be assuaged by having him killed? Or had she, improbably, truly fallen in love with Father Nick—such things did happen, after all—and in the blindness that that love had induced had followed his instructions unthinkingly, mindless of the cost?

Harry might never know. He might not even want to know. But there was no question in his mind that she had long ago overstepped those bounds of forgiveness.

At dusk, when the sky had turned from a faint amber to a smudged gray-blue, Harry got into his car and headed on the winding road that led up into the hillside. He stopped only when he came to the house whose address Keepnews had provided him with.

"It'll be well guarded," Keepnews had told him, and from the looks of it, he'd been right.

The house was set into the hill, propped up over the reach by stilts. A wall of pink stucco fronted on the road and except for four shuttered windows on the second floor, the wall was unbroken, in keeping with the need for security. To gain access it was necessary to go around to the side and there, casually positioned in the shadows, Harry could make out the form of a man. He was leaning indolently against the door, from time to time exchanging remarks with another guard who could not be detected from the street.

In the surrounding bushes, all of which were beautifully manicured and shaped, Harry guessed that there would be other men, armed and awaiting any threat to Father Nick.

Now that Harry was here, he had really no idea what he could do. No plan presented itself to him. He decided that he would merely watch and see what, if anything, happened inside the house or out. Maybe an inspiration would come to him, maybe this whole enterprise was futile and he'd be sensible enough to turn around and go home and forget it. Though the one thing he couldn't see himself doing was forgetting.

Past eleven o'clock, after hours of inaction, a gray

Mercedes appeared in Harry's rearview mirror. Instead of passing him it pulled off the road and stopped. If Harry had had any doubts about the car there was no question about the identity of its owner. It was Harold Keepnews.

He must have noticed Harry's car parked ahead of his but if he did he gave no indication of it. Harry had a good notion of what Keepnews was up to, and he didn't like it at all. Keepnews had decided to employ the same strategy with Father Nick that he had with the burglar who'd once invaded his house. He was going to meet the challenger head on and if necessary, kill him or else die himself. In his state of mind, it probably made very little difference. Love can kill a man more easily than hatred.

That he had given Harry the address of Father Nick's Sausalito hideaway, however, implied that he hadn't lost all reason. It might just be that he wanted back-up, that he expected Harry to be around when he arrived. More than that, he was undoubtedly shrewd enough to realize that Harry was the sort of man who would be unable to stay out of something like this, no matter what his reservations.

Harry cursed Keepnews silently. He did not like others choosing his battleground for him. But it seemed that people were always doing that regardless.

Now he could not imagine Keepnews simply going up to the door and demanding admission. On the other hand, he couldn't imagine him creeping silently among the shadows and ambushing his foes either. But, as he watched with growing shock, that was exactly what Keepnews appeared to have in mind.

As soon as he got within sight of the house he slipped out a .45-caliber combat pistol with a Teflon finish, equipped with a silencer. It was possible that he had already reconnoitered the site, for he seemed to know exactly where to find the guards—the first few at least.

He was going about this operation with a military flourish. Obviously, the consequences of what he was doing were of little significance to him; he had probably not thought this through. Once he got Wendy back, if he

186

got Wendy back, he would worry about everything else.

Harry quietly slid out of his car and darted to the other side of the street, keeping as low as possible for fear of being spied from the house.

Keepnews was less cautious. He slipped up to the door so silently that the man there was caught by surprise. "What do you want?" he managed to say before Keepnews fired his .45 into his face. The guard crumpled against the door and flopped down on the doormat, blotting out the WELCOME printed on it with the blood and brain tissue that rushed out of the jagged wound where his nose had been.

But though he made very little noise in his dying it was still enough to alert the man's colleague, who appeared from around back. Keepnews as soon as he glimpsed him shot him. This guard, however, did not relinquish his hold on life so easily. He shrieked in torment and gripping the wound that lay just under his heart, ran around to the side, seeking another door into the house where he might find help.

His cries drew two more men who materialized out of the high bushes, both carrying automatics. Keepnews crouched and brought the first down, sending him tumbling back into the bushes where he struggled for several moments against the entangling branches, an activity that hastened the flow of arterial blood out of his body that much faster.

The second, with no time to aim, lay down a barrage of automatic fire that carved out an ugly trail in the oaken door over Keepnews' head. Before he could lower his sight, Harry appeared and fired his Magnum into the man's arm, forcing the automatic from his hands. Keepnews unconcernedly put another bullet in him, which eliminated his opposition—and life—immediately.

At that point the door flew open and a burst of fire spewed forth. Whoever was doing the shooting had not taken the trouble to determine where it was he was directing his fire. Harold was just about underfoot, a location he was quick to take advantage of by wheeling

187

about and discharging his .45 into the defender's chest.

Very suddenly there was silence. Keepnews drew himself up and, in a gesture that seemed completely incongruous, dusted off his pants. He raised his eyes toward Harry. He smiled but said nothing. To Harry he looked hypnotized, only marginally conscious of his circumstances. The man had become so obsessed, so exhilarated by the momentum of the battle that he seemed incapable of reacting in any normal manner. Harry wanted to stop him, but no sooner had he uttered Keepnews' name than he'd vanished, rushing up a set of stairs into the darkness. Harry was in no hurry, having no idea what was waiting for him in the dark. It was just possible that Father Nick and Wendy were not at home, that only the security guards were present—or had been until their untimely ends. The problem was that from the exterior you could not tell whether any lights were on inside.

Ahead of him, as he ascended the stairs, Harry heard the rattle of gunfire. There was a cry, then more fire. Harry clung to the walls and reaching the summit, dropped to his knees. A light flashed on, momentarily blinding him. When he could see again, he saw Keepnews sprawled out on the carpeted floor.

He moved, then picked himself up slowly. Beyond him were two additional bodies, both in plainclothes; no telling who they were. Keepnews, inattentive to the possibility of further gunfire, drew fully erect. Seeing Harry, he shrugged apologetically. Blood soaked his shirtfront. When he moved, he moved with difficulty. Harry realized he'd been badly injured, but this evidently wasn't sufficient to stop him.

"All right," he mumbled, "I'm all right, don't you worry." He gestured into what might have been the dining room, which was only partially visible in the dimness. "Must find Wendy, must find her."

Harry thought of a new tack. He clasped Keepnews by the shoulders and urged him to be seated on the couch. "I'll find her for you," he said.

Keepnews shook his head vehemently and got up

again, brushing Harry aside. "My business, my business," he kept saying as he lurched forward into the next room.

Then another light came on—from a chandelier, which provided for elegant illumination as its crystals shimmered with a thousand irridescent colors that glimmered in turn on the smooth rosewood surface of the dining-room table below it. The table was laid out for a dinner of twelve. Where the other eleven diners had gone to, whether they would appear at all for what was obviously supposed to be a late-night supper, was a question Harry would never know the answer to. But the twelfth diner wasn't afraid of showing himself.

It was Father Nick himself, a Baretta 7 in his hand: an ironic touch as Baretta 7s were favored by off-duty police officers.

Harry hung well in back, out of Father Nick's sight. Keepnews demonstrated no such compunction. He must have believed he was already dying because he didn't do anything to protect himself.

Father Nick, however, was somewhat more wary. He had not moved from behind the partition that separated the dining room from what lay beyond it. Only part of his face could be discerned. And the protrusion of the Baretta.

Keepnews seemed unaware of the risk he was taking as he walked—tottered was more like it—in Father Nick's direction. Father Nick, not being one for wasting words, raised his gun to better sight it on Keepnews.

At that moment Harry made his presence known. "Harold!" he shouted. Keepnews turned, but so did Father Nick who fired at Harry. Keepnews in turn fired at Father Nick.

He did not succeed in hitting him, but he did cause him to expose himself just enough for Harry to risk his final round.

The .44 bullet entered Father Nick's skull at a point just above his left eyebrow. When it exited, it flung against the back wall a thick spattering of his brains to which bone chips adhered tenaciously.

Father Nick's left eye filled up with blood, but his right still seemed to apprehend his situation with clarity. He collapsed at Harold Keepnews' feet, his arms outstretched like a supplicant.

Keepnews regarded him with a disdainful eye. He then turned to Harry, scowling. "You should have saved him for me," he said in a low voice.

"You couldn't have gotten him, Harold, he would have killed you."

Keepnews wasn't listening. "Water under the bridge," he mumbled, his breathing becoming more difficult now; he was nearly in shock.

"We need to get you to a hospital."

"No, no, must find Wendy," he said. This objective mobilized him so much that he was already racing away from Harry, leaving a sad trail of blood in his wake.

Harry caught up with him without much problem. If he wasn't going to quit this madness, he thought, he'd just have to help him. Taking his arm he guided Keepnews up the stairs. Keepnews seemed to know where he was going; Harry certainly didn't.

Where he was going, it appeared, was the bedroom. Father Nick's bedroom. A nicely appointed place. A fine blue bedspread over the large double bed with a canopy overhead and a mirror on the underside of the canopy so that you could see how you were progressing with your lady or gentleman friend, depending on your sex and your proclivities. And on the bed, clad in a nightgown that precisely matched the bedspread and that had been hiked up almost to her waist to exhibit those beautiful tan legs of hers, was Wendy Keepnews. She was crying and that, more than anything else this night, astounded Harry, who had never thought he would see her like this. She was crying softly into a crumpled Kleenex. Her eyes were red, when you could see them—mostly she kept her face hidden by the damp strands of her hair. Her whole body shook with sobbing.

"Wendy, Wendy, Wendy," Keepnews said, throwing himself on the bed, reaching out his hands for hers.

"Forgive me, sweetheart, forgive me!" he pleaded though Harry wasn't sure it shouldn't have been the other way around. She didn't look at him.

He repeated her name twice, three times more, like a litany. Then he couldn't any longer. He ran out of strength for words. He took her hand in his. She didn't resist and clutched it fervently. But not so fervently. He'd run out of strength, he'd run out of life. His life was in the blood and it was all over the blue bedspread. Wendy didn't react, might not have realized he was gone, she couldn't stop her crying.

Harry found the phone. It was blue too, matching precisely as well.

He dialed his department and asked for Bob Togan.

Togan was at his desk. "Harry? Is that you? I've been trying to get ahold of you for days. What happened to you?" He didn't wait for an answer, rushing headlong into the next sentence. "I've got good news. The Internal Affairs committee met on your case, and the word is it looks good for you. Pending your personal testimony, they felt you should be restored to the department with no problem. Maybe collect all your back pay. This Father Nick business seems to be all over and done with."

Harry smiled painfully. "This Father Nick business is all over and done with, Bob, but not in quite the way you mean."

"Don't tell me . . . not again?"

"You know where Cimentini lives?"

Togan said that he did. "Is that where you are now?"

"You call up the boys in Sausalito, tell them to get over here. You might want to join them. I don't think they're up to this sort of thing."

"Shit, Harry. Why the hell are you always getting into these messes? Can you tell me that?"

"See you shortly, Bob," Harry said, ignoring the question. He put down the phone and turned to the woman crying on the bed. "Now, Mrs. Keepnews, you and I are going to have a little talk."

THE BEST OF ADVENTURE
by RAMSAY THORNE

RENEGADE #1:   (C90-976, $1.95)
RENEGADE #2:   BLOOD RUNNER   (C90-977, $1.95)
RENEGADE #3:   FEAR MERCHANT   (C90-761, $1.95)
RENEGADE #4:   DEATH HUNTER   (C90-902, $1.95)
RENEGADE #5:   MACUMBA KILLER   (C90-234, $1.95)
RENEGADE #6:   PANAMA GUNNER   (C90-235, $1.95)
RENEGADE #7:   DEATH IN
               HIGH PLACES   (C90-548, $1.95)
RENEGADE #8:   OVER THE ANDES
               TO HELL   (C90-549, $1.95)
RENEGADE #9:   HELL RAIDER   (C90-550, $1.95)
RENEGADE #10: THE GREAT GAME   (C90-737, $1.95)
RENEGADE #11: CITADEL OF DEATH   (C90-738, $1.95)
RENEGADE #12: THE BADLANDS
               BRIGADE   (C90-739, $1.95)

To order, use the coupon below. If you prefer to use your
own stationery, please include complete title as well as
book number and price. Allow 4 weeks for delivery.